Praise for *15 Days Without a Head*

"A fine book. Laurence and Jay are so sensitively and sweetly imagined that I wanted to rush round to Parkview Heights myself, to give them a hug and a bag of chips!"

—Julie Hearn, author of *Rowan the Strange*

"An excellent debut. It's a tough and turbulent tale of growing up the hard way, but there's heart and soul on every page. I can't wait to see what Cousins does next."

—Keith Gray, author of *Ostrich Boys*

"Unputdownable—heart-warming and heartbreaking at the same time, with the most loveable and memorable characters. A jewel of a book!"

—Candy Gourlay, author of *Tall Story*

"Dave Cousins' fantastic writing laces a tough tale with humor, warmth, and a cast of beautifully depicted characters."

—Paula Rawsthorne, author of
The Truth about Celia Frost

15 DAYS

With-out a

HEAD

For Jane, Ptolemy, Hockey,
and Dylan, with love.

15 DAYS With-out a HEAD

Dave Cousins

flux
™
Woodbury, Minnesota

15 Days Without a Head © 2013 by Dave Cousins. All rights reserved. No part of this book may be used or reproduced in any manner whatsoever, including Internet usage, without written permission from Flux, except in the case of brief quotations embodied in critical articles and reviews.

First U.S. Edition
First Printing, 2013

Originally published by Oxford University Press, Oxford, UK, 2012

Book design by Bob Gaul
Cover design by Lisa Novak
Cover images: Telephone booth © iStockphoto.com/Lucia Chacon
            Boy © Image Source/PunchStock

Flux, an imprint of Llewellyn Worldwide Ltd.

This is a work of fiction. Names, characters, places, and incidents are either the product of the author's imagination or are used fictitiously, and any resemblance to actual persons living or dead, business establishments, events, or locales is entirely coincidental. Cover model used for illustrative purposes only and may not endorse or represent the book's subject.

Library of Congress Cataloging-in-Publication Data
Cousins, Dave.
  15 days without a head/Dave Cousins.—First U.S. edition.
      pages cm
  "Originally published by Oxford University Press, 2012"—Copyright page.
  Summary: When his alcoholic mother disappears, fifteen-year-old Laurence is determined to find her, take care of his little brother, and keep their predicament a secret, all while trying to win a luxury vacation for his mom in a radio call-in contest.
  ISBN 978-0-7387-3642-6
  [1. Abandoned children—Fiction. 2. Alcoholism—Fiction. 3. Mothers—Fiction. 4. Contests—Fiction.] I. Title. II. Title: Fifteen days without a head.
  PZ7.C831747Aah 2013
  [Fic]—dc23
                                                    2012048953

Flux
Llewellyn Worldwide Ltd.
2143 Wooddale Drive
Woodbury, MN 55125-2989
www.fluxnow.com

Printed in the United States of America

Acknowledgments

Writing a book can take a long time and is, for the most part, a solitary venture. But I would like to acknowledge the help and support I have received from a number of people, without whom *15 Days Without a Head* would never have been published.

My greatest debt is owed to my family (Cousins and Raven) and friends, for their tolerance, encouragement, and patience. My wife Jane read each draft many times and never held back from giving an honest opinion. Other early readers, my mum Pam Cousins and Tony and Viv Martin, gave me valuable feedback, while Helen Corner at Cornerstones told me I should keep going. A special thank you to EDMTC for her never-ending faith, and for buying me a computer to write this on. Love and thanks to Ptol, Hock, and Dylan for inspiration, and for reminding me of what's really important.

Gratitude to Patti Wright-Goss for putting me in touch with Eilis Woodlock, whose experience as a Children's Social Worker was invaluable. Thumbs-up to Mike Bouvier and Nick Harper for setting me straight on the workings of a local radio phone-in, and many thanks to my dad, Mike Cousins, for sharing his inside knowledge of the day-to-day operation of secondary schools and for checking my Shakespeare.

Natascha Biebow, Sara Grant, and Sara O'Connor at SCBWI in the UK will eternally be my fairy godmothers for organizing the inspired *Undiscovered Voices* anthology and changing my life forever. Ann Tobias was generous with her time and advice, and I am privileged to work with Sarah Manson, probably the best agent in the world, and to benefit from her insight, belief, and enthusiasm. Sarah, alongside my wonderful editor Jasmine Richards, and everyone at Oxford University Press must take the credit for making a dream come true when they published this story in the UK.

The book you are holding today would not exist if Brian Farrey-Latz had not brought Laurence, Jay, and Mina to the United States. I am hugely grateful to everyone at Flux, especially Brian, Sandy, Bob, Lisa, Courtney, and Mallory for all their hard work in making sure my book would become better traveled than I am!

Finally, thanks to you, the reader, for picking up a copy. I hope you enjoy the story.

Dave Cousins
Hertfordshire, England
February 2013

TUESDAY

The front door slams. Mum's back.

It sounds like a dead body hitting the ground as she dumps her stuff in the hall and goes straight to the kitchen. I hear the thud of a bottle on the table, the crack of the cap, then the slow glug as liquid spills into a glass.

Mum coughs, drags a chair across the floor, and sits down.

The smell of cigarette smoke drifts into the front room, where me and Jay are being quiet. Keeping out of the way until Happy Hour—when the first drink has worked its magic and made her smile again.

"Where are my beautiful boys? Where are they hiding?"

That's the signal, the all clear; it's safe to go out there. Happy Hour has begun.

We go into the kitchen. Jay runs into her arms and she's all smiles and kisses. I hang back by the door until she waves me over and pulls me into the hug. The smell of chip fat and cigarettes is suffocating.

Jay tells her about his day at school. She listens and smiles and refills the glass. The liquid inside is thick and red.

Slowly she stops listening. Her eyes glaze over and the

smile sags. Jay's still talking, his high, six-year-old voice too loud. There's a knife on the table and he's spinning it while he talks. "And then at playtime, Matt said…" *swish* "…but we didn't want to play that…" *swish, clink* "…so I said we should play…" *clink, swish, tink* as it clips the bottle and Mum's eye starts to twitch.

I put my hand over the knife and tell Jay it's time for bed.

He scowls at me. "Not going to bed."

"Yes you are, it's bedtime."

"Not!"

"Come on, Jay."

"It's not up to you anyway." He looks at Mum.

Her eyes stumble back into focus. "What's that, sweetheart?"

"I don't have to go to bed, do I?"

"Of course not, darling. Come and give Mummy a cuddle."

My little brother gives me a triumphant look and clambers into her lap. I shrug and leave them to it. But I stay within earshot.

Happy Hour lasts for approximately one hour. Sometimes less. It's worse when she doesn't drink, when we've run out of money. No drink equals no Happy Hour. Mum storming round the flat, shouting at me and Jay because everything's in a mess. Either that or she stays in bed all day, or locks herself in the bathroom and you can hear her crying through the door. Sometimes she's in there for hours, so I have to take Jay outside to wee behind the bins.

I get Jay into his pajamas by eight o'clock. He shuffles along the hall to the bathroom on all fours, then looks back at me and barks. This is perfectly normal behavior—at least, it's not unusual for Jay. I don't remember when his thing with dogs began, but he only started pretending he was one just after we moved here. He doesn't do it all the time, just when he knows it's going to wind me up—like now.

"Come on, Jay, do your teeth."

I squirt some toothpaste onto his toothbrush and offer it to him.

He shakes his head.

"If you don't do your teeth they'll fall out."

Jay woofs and grins up at me.

We haven't got time for this. If Mum finds out he's not in bed yet, she'll go gorilla on us.

"Come on, get up!" I grab his arm and try to pull him to his feet.

Jay growls and sinks his teeth into my wrist.

I drop the toothbrush in surprise.

"You bit me!" It doesn't hurt, but he's left a perfect imprint of his teeth in my skin.

Jay looks at me, and there's a glint of a smile in his eyes.

Now I'm mad.

"Right!" This time I pick him up by the shoulders and dump him on his feet. Jay twists and squirms, trying to bite me again, but I'm too strong for him and he knows it. I pick up the toothbrush and push it to his lips. He glares at me, mouth clamped shut, cheeks flaming. Then suddenly, his face crumples and he starts to cry.

I panic—try to put my arms round him—anything to stop the noise.

That sound is one of the few things that will penetrate the Cloud. The Cloud is what follows Happy Hour, and it lasts a lot longer. A force-field of cigarette smoke and booze, with our mum inside. It reminds me of that old TV program *Stars in Their Eyes*—when the contestant goes through the door as one person, then emerges from the smoke looking completely different. Except in Mum's case, she comes out looking exactly the same—it's her personality that's changed. I don't suppose that would make much of a TV show, though.

I hear her coming now, crashing down the hall like King Kong, swearing as she bounces off the walls.

"What the hell's going on in here?"

For a second Jay stops crying. His eyes widen, but he's still too young to hear the warning in her voice. He starts blubbing again and points at me.

"Lau—rence—hurt—my arm."

Mum snatches Jay's toothbrush from me and thrusts it in my face. "For God's sake! Can't you do anything without making a fuss?" Her tongue has gone black and her breath makes my stomach twitch.

She's waiting for an answer, but how do you reply to a question like that? So I shrug. Bad choice. Mum hates it when I shrug. I make a mental note to try and remember in future, right before she slaps me, hard across the face.

"*Don't* shrug at me!"

"Sorry."

She shoves the toothbrush at Jay. "Clean your teeth and get to bed—both of you. I'm sick of the sight of you."

It's five past eight. I'm fifteen, and I'm being sent to bed at five past eight.

Jay starts brushing his teeth. He won't look at me.

My face stings and I can feel the skin around my eye starting to swell. It's my own fault. I should have known what would happen.

I lie on Jay's bed and read him a story. He's forgiven me for the Great Teeth Cleaning Incident. I think he feels guilty because Mum slapped me.

"You were crying," he says.

"It wasn't crying. It just stung a bit. Sometimes your eyes water, but it's not the same as crying."

"Didn't it hurt?"

"Nah, not really," I lie.

There are stars on the ceiling in our room. They used to glow in the dark. When Mum stuck them up, she copied real constellations from a book in the library. She decorated the whole flat when we moved here, painted each room a different color. There was this horrible brown flowery wallpaper in the front room, and one night Mum just started tearing it off the wall in big strips. I thought she'd gone mad. Then me and Jay joined in. The three of us dancing round the front room with Mum's Queen CD on full-blast, chucking bits of wallpaper into the air until it was swirling round us like a snow storm.

That was ages ago. When Mum was still trying.

Moving here was supposed to be a fresh start—a place where nobody knew us, a place with no history.

We live on the top floor of a building called Parkview Heights—which is a stupid name because it's only three stories high and the view is of the car park. It looms like a tombstone over the actual park, the one with the grass and the trees. The ground level is occupied by a line of dingy shops, laughingly called Parkview Parade. The two floors above contain equally dingy flats, accessed by an exterior flight of stone steps and a set of double doors with metal bars over the glass. When we moved in, I assumed they were there to keep people out; now I'm not so sure. There's a saying round here that goes: *How do you know when you've hit rock bottom?* Answer: *You wake up in the Heights!* We've got cockroaches in the kitchen and the toilet leaks— and if you open any of the windows, the smell from the fish and chip shop in the Parade stinks the place out.

But it's all we can afford. Mum's too scared to apply for benefits in case they trace us back to Bridgewell and start asking questions. When people start asking questions, they don't always like the answers you give, and that's when things get scary.

Like last time—when the woman with the clipboard came round and said it would be best if me and Jay went to live with someone else, just while Mum got back on her feet. That was approximately ten seconds before Mum threw her out. The same night we were on a train coming here—the Incredible Disappearing Family. I wondered what the kids at school would think when I just vanished, then realized that half of them probably wouldn't even notice. To think that you could leave somewhere and nobody would even realize you'd gone, because they'd never noticed you were there in the first place. That's hard.

The Scooby-Doo alarm clock next to the bed says 08:55 p.m. It's time.

I check that Jay is asleep, then reach under my mattress and pull out the envelope with the phonecards inside. Mum stole them from the newsagent's shop where she used to work. She'd still kill me if she found out I'd nicked a load from her, though. Free phone calls, Mum said, but she never used them because she couldn't be bothered to walk to a phone box. We both had mobiles at the time anyway, until Mum lost hers and pinched mine. That was months ago. I haven't seen her with it for ages, so she probably lost that one too. She said she'd buy me a new one when she gets a better job, but I'm not holding my breath. Until then, at least I've got these.

I slip the cards into the back pocket of my jeans and open the window. The air is thick like custard and smells of frying fish. I lever myself up onto the sill and swing my legs through the gap. I wait a moment, feeling the heat close around me, then let myself slide.

Directly outside our bedroom window, the roof of the floor below forms a two-meter ledge that runs the length of the building. The surface looks like melted gray cheese, and smells like electricity in the heat. Black sticky stuff oozes from cracks around the edges, and if you get any on your hands it leaves a brown stain for days.

I walk along to the end of the roof, then turn round. This is the bit I hate—lowering myself over the edge. I feel with my feet for the fire escape bolted to the side of the building—rickety steps of rusty metal that boom and rattle under me. There's a chain across the flight down to street level, so I climb over the side, onto one of the big bins lining the access road behind the shops. I check that there's nobody around, then jump down.

So far I've been lucky. I don't think about what will happen when my luck runs out. It could be tonight. I tell myself it doesn't matter. If I don't care too much I'll be OK. Most of all, I don't think about what Mum would say if she knew what I was doing. Leaving Jay on his own with her is a risk, especially in the mood she's in tonight, but I have to do this—for all our sakes.

Most of the shops in the Parade have their shutters down, but SavaShoppa, the launderette, and the off-licence are still open. I cross the car park to the telephone box and pull open the door—a smell of wee and cigarettes steps out to greet me. I'm shaking already, but that's normal. The thing is not to think about what you're doing—just do it.

I lift the heavy receiver and check that nobody has left chewing gum on the earpiece or spat in the end, then fish one of Mum's hot phonecards from my pocket and punch in the code. I know the number off by heart. I dial and listen to the buzz in my ear, waiting for somebody to answer.

There's graffiti sprayed all over the glass walls of the phone box, but I can see the windows of our flat through the gaps. If Mum looked out she'd be able to see me—but she won't. She thinks I'm in my room, in bed. She won't move until she's run out of booze, and I'll be back long before that happens. Unless Jay wakes up ... but I can't think about that right now.

A cheery female voice answers the phone, and I'm on.

If I don't think about being on the radio, it's OK. It's just me and Baz the DJ, having a conversation. He's asking me some questions, that's all. I'm not live on-air, pretending to be my dad and trying to win a luxury holiday.

What I have to remember is to keep the voice going. You have to be eighteen to play, which is why I'm impersonating my dad—don't worry, he won't find out: he's dead. His name was Daniel, and he didn't actually have a Scottish accent, but I wanted to disguise my voice so I'm using my impression of Mr. Buchan, our Head of Year at school. The people at the radio station seem to believe me so far, and this is my third day.

Baz is talking to the listeners, getting ready to introduce me. I wish he'd get on with it. It's the waiting I can't stand.

"Welcome back to our current champion, Daniel Roach! How you doing, Dan? D'you feel lucky? That's what you gotta ask yourself—DO YOU FEEL LUCKY?"

That's how he says it—in capital letters. I don't feel lucky. My legs are shaking and I need to go to the toilet.

"Pretty lucky." I shrug, but it doesn't matter—this is radio.

"PRETTY LUCKY?" repeats Baz. "Well, let's see if pretty lucky will be enough to keep Daniel in the game. Remember—ALL he has to do is answer three questions correctly and he'll be one step closer to that all-expensespaid family holiday, courtesy of our friends at Hardacre Holidaze." The Hardacre Holidaze jingle chimes down the phone—*Not just a holiday, the best daze of your life!*

"So … Danny boy, it's in YOUR HANDS, fella—no pressure!" Baz pauses for effect, or maybe he's waiting for me to answer.

My mouth has gone dry.

"Daniel," says Baz. "Are you ready?"

I lick my lips. "Yeah."

"First question."

A car screams past outside, stereo blaring.

"The First World War ended in which year? Was it A: 1945? B: 1918? Or C: 1939? I'll read those again. The First World War ended in WHICH year of our Lord? Was it A: 1945? B: 1918? Or C: 1939?"

I breathe out. It must sound like a hurricane on the air. "B: 1918."

Silence from Baz. "That's the FIRST World War, Danny.

And you're saying it ended, finished, packed up and went home in 1918?"

"Yes." I know I'm right. We did the First World War in Year Nine. Or was that the Second World War? I go cold. Suddenly I'm not sure.

"CORRECT!" says Baz, and I can almost hear him grinning. "A nice easy one to start you off there, Dan! Bit of a historian, are you?"

"Not really. We did it at school," I say without thinking.

Baz laughs. "I probably did too—but I find it hard remembering what I did YESTERDAY! In fact, if anybody can TELL ME what I was doing yesterday, give me a call!"

I could kick myself for being so careless. I'm supposed to be a forty-year-old man—I don't go to school anymore!

"A GOOD start from our champion!" says Baz. "You obviously know your history, Daniel, but what are you like on sport?"

"OK," I tell Baz, but I'm lying. I know nothing about sport.

"That's a pity," he says, "because this next question . . . is a MUSIC one!" He laughs and triggers one of his famous sound effects. "Sorry, fella—not really TRYING to put you off!" He's still chuckling to himself as he asks the question. "Daniel, which of these three was NOT in the legendary pop group the Beatles? Was it A: Richard Starkey? B: Pete Best? Or C: Julian Lennon? Are you a Beatles FAN, DAN?"

"They're OK." My mouth has gone dry again. I don't know the answer, but I think it's a trick question. I've not heard of any of them, but the only one that sounds like one of the Beatles is C ... but it was *John* Lennon, not Julian ... at least I think it was.

"You still with us, champ?"

"Yeah."

"I'm going to have to HURRY you for an answer."

I swallow. "C: Julian Lennon." The moment it's out, I know I'm wrong.

Baz sighs. "Let me get this right, Dan. You're telling me that C—Julian Lennon—was NOT one of the fabulous Mersey Mop Tops? Is that right?"

"Yeah." There's no point asking if I can take it back. It's in the rules. They have to take your first answer. I'm an idiot.

"You're absolutely CORRECT!" says Baz, as the sound of taped applause fills the studio. "Richard Starkey, better known as Ringo Starr, and Pete Best BOTH drummed for the Fab Four. Julian is, as Danny knows, John Lennon's son, but NEVER ACTUALLY PLAYED with the band. Well done, Dan! See—I told you it was easy!"

"Yeah," I say, wiping the sweat off my forehead.

"Just one more and you're through," says Baz, his voice low in my ear. "Daniel. Are you ready?"

"Ready."

"Question number three."

A light goes on in the flat above the chip shop and I can see the flicker of the TV in the window of our front room.

"What do you call the small pieces of colored paper we throw into the air at weddings? Is it A: confetti? B: papyrus? Or C: paprika?"

"Confetti. A."

"Whoa! Quick off the mark with THAT one, Daniel! Something tells ME that you've been to a wedding recently!"

"No."

"But you're married yourself, right?"

Just in time, I remember to say "Yeah"—and realize I just told the thousand or so people listening that I'm married to my own mother.

"How long?"

"What?"

Baz laughs. "How long have you and the lovely Mrs. Roach been married? Don't tell me you've FORGOTTEN? I hope she's not listening to this, Daniel, or you're going to be in TROUBLE tonight, my friend!"

He doesn't know how right he is.

"No, she's not ... I hope." That's the first honest word I've said all night.

"You could well be in LUCK, my friend," says Baz. "Because you are quite correct! People DO NOT throw paprika or papyrus at a wedding—at least they don't where I come from. Rocks and bottles sometimes, but never PAPRIKA! Imagine trying to get THAT out of your frock! No, when people go to weddings, they do in fact throw CONFETTI. WHICH MEANS, Daniel my friend, that you are still in the game!" The *Baz's Bedtime Bonanza* theme music starts to play in the background. "SO, I'll see YOU—

HERE—TOMORROW NIGHT! SAME TIME—SAME
PLACE—RADIO HAM on the medium wave..."

I heave open the door of the phone box and take a gulp
of air. I'm soaked in sweat, but I can't help grinning. I did
it. Three down, only seven more to go. If I can stay in for
ten days I'll win the holiday. If there's anything that's going
to cheer Mum up enough to stop her drinking, it's a two-
week, all-expenses-paid holiday in the sun.

WHENSDAY

A distorted blast of music wrenches me from sleep. I reach out and slam my hand down on the Scooby-Doo alarm clock beside the bed, and let the silence hang…

The flickering red digits read 05:01 a.m. Across the room, Jay grunts and mumbles but doesn't wake up. The flat is silent. My eyes close for no more than a second, but somehow the clock now says 05:07 a.m. I swing my legs over the side of the bed and stand up—still asleep, but moving.

I switch on the light in the kitchen and the cockroaches scatter for cover. *Roaches for Roaches!* Mum always says— she thinks it's funny, what with our name being Roach.

It's a joke all right, but that doesn't make it funny.

I pull a cup from the dirty stack in the sink, rinse it, and wait for the kettle to boil.

As well as working at the chip shop in the Parade, Mum does a dawn shift cleaning offices on the industrial estate across town. She has to be there by six thirty, but if she's been drinking the night before—which is pretty much every night—she doesn't get up. Mum needs both jobs to earn enough to pay the rent, which is why every morning I have to get up at five o'clock to make sure she gets out of bed.

Some days she won't get up at all and I have to do the shift for her. It doesn't matter which one of us goes, so long as somebody swipes the little plastic card through the machine to prove she's been there. If the offices get cleaned, Mum gets paid. So long as Mum gets paid, we have food to eat and a place to live. *We all live here, so why shouldn't we all help pay for it?* Mum says, and you can't really argue with that. But then, arguing with Mum about anything is a bad idea.

I put two spoons of coffee powder into the mug and stir in the water: Mum likes her coffee strong. There's no milk, so I add extra sugar and then take the cup along the hall.

Mum's bedroom door is shut. I knock and turn the handle.

The smell of booze hits me like a burp.

"Mum?"

She's asleep with her mouth open, still wearing most of her clothes.

I weave my way through the debris on the floor and put the mug by the bed.

"Mum? Mum!"

It's a waste of time. I know she won't answer—there are two empty wine bottles on the kitchen table.

I get the urge to dump the coffee over her head, but I'm not sure even that would wake her up. Instead I switch on the radio, turn up the volume, and leave.

I crawl back into bed and listen to the noise through the wall. It stops abruptly and Mum shouts something. I don't catch exactly what she says, but the meaning is clear enough. I lie in the dark waiting, listening to Mum slam around; then finally the door bangs shut and I can breathe again. She won't be back until after me and Jay have left for school.

There's no point trying to go back to sleep, even though I'm so tired I feel sick. So I go to the kitchen, scrape the mold off another cup, and make myself a coffee with extra sugar. Then I slip out onto the roof to watch the sun come up.

Mum's been sick in the bathtub. I have to wash the dark brown ooze away before I can have a shower. The smell twists my stomach and sends the bittersweet taste of coffee back up my throat. There's no soap so I wash myself in shampoo, standing under the water until it goes cold.

When I turn off the taps I can hear the TV, which means Jay must be up. I wrap a towel around my waist and follow the sound to the front room. It's an episode of *Scooby-Doo*. Cannibals are chasing Shaggy and Scooby across an island and Jay's laughing so much he almost falls off the settee. I tell him to come and get dressed.

We need to go to the launderette. I sniff the three school shirts strewn across the floor and choose one that doesn't smell quite as bad as the others, then give my armpits an extra spray.

There's nothing to eat for breakfast, so I take two pounds

from the scatter of coins on Mum's dressing table. We can stop at the shop on the way to school.

Nosy Nelly is waiting for us as we cross the lobby, though she pretends it's a coincidence. She's still wearing a dressing gown, with her ridiculous dyed-black hair smothered beneath a hairnet. Her real name is Mrs. Ellison and she lives in flat number one, by the main door. Whenever you go in or out she's there and she knows everything about everyone.

"Good morning, boys!" Nelly smiles like a dog—all yellow teeth and gums.

I nod, and Jay just stares at her. But Nelly likes Jay—everybody does. He's one of those blond, angelic-looking kids that strangers coo over. Lots of people mistake him for a girl because he's so pretty. That gets him mad, but it makes me laugh.

Nelly bends down and shoves her face into his. "Aren't you a lucky boy, having your big brother walk you to school!"

Jay shrugs. "He's not my full brother, he's my half brother, because his dad's not the same as my dad."

I wince. Nelly's going to love that juicy piece of information. Mum'll go ape if she finds out he told her—not that Nelly couldn't have worked it out for herself. Jay and me look nothing alike. If Jay's the kid people smile at in the street, I'm the one they cross the road to avoid. I'm over six feet tall, for a start, and there's something about my face that makes people uneasy. It's as though my features don't quite go together, like clothes that don't match. Imagine one of those composite mug shots the police put out on TV, add a frame of mud-brown curly hair, and you'll get the picture.

"Mummy having a lie-in, is she?" Nelly's voice is all syrup, but I know where she's leading.

"She's at work," says Jay. Of course Nelly already knows this—she's had the front door staked out since dawn.

"I hope you boys have been behaving yourselves, all on your own upstairs?" She looks at me as she says it.

I avoid her eyes and grab Jay's hand, pulling him towards the door. "Come on, Jay, we're going to be late."

"You're hurting!"

"Well come on then!"

Outside, he twists himself free. "You didn't have to pull my arm off!"

I don't answer, but when we get to the shop I let him choose what he wants for breakfast, as compensation. He grins and hands me a packet of Pickled Onion Monster Munch.

We sit on the wall at the end of the Parade and share a can of lemonade. It's still early but I can feel the heat closing in already, making my armpits prickle.

A bus goes past with kids on it from my school, which means it's time to go.

I nudge Jay. "You ready, Monster Boy?"

He scowls. "I'm not a monster!"

"Are."

"Not! If I was, I wouldn't be eating these." He waves the Monster Munch at me.

"Why not?"

"It's Monster Munch. I'd be canniballing!"

I laugh, even though he's deadly serious.

"If there's no food again tonight, will we have to be cannibals and find somebody to eat?" he asks, quite matter-of-fact, as we walk down the hill to school.

"Maybe."

He thinks about this. "I wouldn't like to eat Nosy Nelly."

I laugh. I wouldn't want to eat her either, but I wouldn't mind if someone else did.

Jay's school isn't far. I walk him to the gate and wait until he goes inside, then start to run. Hardacre Comprehensive is on the other side of town. If I'm lucky I'll get there just as the bell goes. Twenty minutes flat-out with a bag of books on your back is bad enough in normal weather, but in this heat!

By the time I get to school, the playground is empty. I've missed registration and assembly has started, so I have to go to the office and sign the Late Book. I make it back just in time to join the queue lining up for first period—out of breath and sweating like a kebab.

It's so hot in here. My legs ache. I can't keep still. At least there's only another half an hour until hometime. I try to focus on what Mr. Buchan is saying, running my finger along the words on the page, but they might as well be hieroglyphics for all they mean to me.

The teacher's voice is warm and rhythmic, the page soft under my fingers. I stop fighting and let my eyelids drop for a moment. This is better. I can still listen with my eyes closed; it's no problem.

I wake up when Mr. Buchan drops the *Complete Works of Shakespeare* onto my desk. For a few seconds I don't know where I am.

"Glad to have you back with us, Laurence!" Buchan's eyebrows twitch.

I don't say anything, just wipe the drool from the corner of my mouth, hoping nobody noticed.

"Maybe you'd like to explain why Macbeth says, *Wicked dreams abuse the curtain'd sleep*? Any recent dreams you'd like to share with us?"

Somebody sniggers.

"No, sir." I can feel all eyes in the room nudging me.

Buchan sighs and shakes his head. "Try to stay with us, Laurence, at least until the end of the lesson."

I nod and turn my burning face back to the page, but the words still mean nothing because now I'm thinking about the Dream. My dream—the one where the woman with the clipboard comes to take Jay away.

It's always the same: Jay in his Scooby-Doo pajamas being carried down the hall. He's screaming my name, reaching out to me, but I can't move. Then I notice there are empty bottles all over the floor. I'm trying to walk through them, but my feet keep slipping on the glass. I realize the floor is no longer solid but an ocean of bottles, bobbing and clanking around me. I'm sinking, drowning. A thick red sea invades my mouth and nostrils, sucking me under until I'm trapped, helpless, as the woman with the clipboard takes Jay away.

That's the part when I wake up.

Sweating.

In the dark.

The bell goes for the end of school but Mr. Buchan asks me to stay behind. I know what's coming. I just hope it won't take too long because I have to collect Jay.

"Looks as if you've been in the wars, lad!" The teacher perches on the edge of the desk opposite and peers at me. "Nice shiner you've got there."

I'd forgotten about my eye.

"I was fighting with my brother." Lying's easy when you do it all the time.

"Must be a big lad, your brother, to put one on you."

That's funny, so I laugh, relax—and make a mistake.

"He's six," I say.

"Six foot?"

"Six years old."

Buchan laughs, so maybe it's OK.

"We were playing—he gets a bit excited sometimes."

Buchan nods and folds his arms. "I take it you're not a fan of Mr. Shakespeare then?"

I shrug. Truth is, I don't mind Shakespeare.

"I know students get bored sometimes, but I think you're the first who's actually fallen asleep on me!"

"Sorry, sir, I didn't mean to."

"I can't say I'm surprised," says Buchan, frowning. "You look awful. When was the last time you had a decent night's rest?"

I feel his eyes probe beyond the skin and bone of my skull, like he can see right into my head. I need to keep talking, distract him so he won't see what's inside—

"The bloke in the flat next door, he's always got his telly on full blast. I think he's deaf or something." I shrug. "It's hard to get to sleep sometimes."

"I can imagine." Buchan strokes his chin. "Could your mother not have a word with him? Explain the noise is keeping you awake."

I nod. "Maybe." My armpits are burning. I can smell the sour stink of sweat, mixed with that stuff I sprayed on this morning.

"I take it that's why you're missing morning registration? Struggling to get up?" Buchan glances at a sheet of paper I didn't notice he was holding. "I've received this memo from your Form Tutor, Miss Connolly; she says you missed morning registration three times last week, and you were late again this morning."

"Sorry." I can't tell him I'm late because I have to take my little brother to school.

"I'm afraid sorry isn't quite good enough, Laurence. Year Ten has a big effect on your GCSE prospects, and you don't want to be getting into bad time-keeping habits with important exams coming up. I'm pleased to say that I've had no complaints about your classwork, and you seem to be getting your homework and assignments in on time, but promptness is an important part of school life, Laurence." Buchan sighs. "As for falling asleep in class—not all of my colleagues would be as understanding as I am."

I nod. Buchan's OK. As our Head of Year, he acts like he might actually care. Trouble is, that makes him dangerous—one of those people who thinks they're helping when really they're making things worse. Much better that nobody notices me. I couldn't care less if I'm invisible to most of them. Invisibility is fine; it's the superpower I'd pick every time. Most people want strength, X-ray vision, or the ability to fly. Not me. Just to be able to fade away—how good would that be?

"I'll try to get up earlier," I tell him, thinking about watching the dawn come up this morning.

Buchan smiles and waves his sheet of paper. "Good idea. Three more strikes on here and I'm afraid we'll have to put you on daily report. That would mean getting a signature from Miss Connolly at registration, and from each of your subject teachers throughout the day. You'd also need to see me with the report at the end of school, and get your mother to sign the card each evening." He folds his arms. "I imagine you could do without the hassle—I know I could. So let's see if we can avoid it, eh?"

I nod. So much for being invisible. Plus, if I have to see Buchan before I leave, I'll be late collecting Jay—which reminds me. "Can I go now?"

"Yes, of course. Get yourself off home. An early night perhaps?"

"Yeah."

"Sleep's important, Laurence, a great healer. As Macbeth says, it *knits up the ravelled sleeve of care* and is *chief nourisher in life's feast.*" He smiles and stands up. "Did you know they use sleep deprivation as a form of torture?"

I shake my head. I didn't know that.

I can feel Buchan watching as I pack away my books, and I know the look that's in his eyes, one that says *I know there's something you're not telling me,* and the smile offering *You can talk to me. I can help.* There's a part of me that wants to tell him. Maybe he could help, make everything better? All I have to do is open my mouth...

I make it into the corridor with my secrets intact. Sweat has glued my shirt to my skin and my heart feels like it's trying to break out of my chest. I take a few deep breaths, then head for the exit. I'm going to have to run all the way to get Jay.

I turn the corner and almost trip over Hanif from my English group.

"Hey, Roach! You OK, man? Buchan give you a hard time?"

I shrug then frown, trying to make my eyebrows meet in the middle like Mr. Buchan's. "I know students get bored sometimes," I say in what is a near-perfect impression of the teacher, "but I think you're the first who's actually fallen asleep on me!"

Han's laugh echoes down the empty corridor. He slaps me on the arm and shakes his head. "That's brilliant! You should be on the telly, man!"

Or on the radio, I think.

I feel bad making fun of Buchan, but what can you do? I've been the new kid in school too many times. Sometimes it helps if you can make people laugh. With a face like mine you've got two choices: hard man or comedian. One fighter in the family is enough.

Han closes his locker and walks beside me. "I can't stick that Shakespeare stuff though, man. I mean, what's that all about?"

"Yeah!" We push through the doors and the heat hits us like a bus.

"Man! It's hot!" Han yanks off his tie and stuffs it into his pocket. "You coming up the Arcade?"

"I can't."

He shrugs. "See you later then, man."

I watch him go, then turn up the hill and start to run, frustration and anger smelting an iron weight in my guts.

You can hear them halfway up the drive: kids shouting their heads off inside the House of Fun. I spot Jay's voice among the others. It seems a shame to take him away, but Mum can only afford to pay the childminder for an hour.

I press the bell and see Angie approaching through the frosted glass: a kaleidoscope of primary colors.

"Hello, Laurence love!" She beams at me, as though I'm the one person in the whole world she hoped would be standing on her doorstep. "Come in, come in!" Then she frowns. "What happened to you?" She means my eye.

"Rugby, at school." I'm such a good liar.

"Rugby? In the summer term?" Or maybe not.

I shrug. "Just a one-off game, interhouse thing."

"Well, I hope you won. I've always thought rugby was a barbaric game." Angie shakes her head. "Let me get you a drink. You must be parched in this heat?"

"No, I'm fine, thanks."

It's the same ritual every time. She offers me a drink, or a biscuit, or a packet of crisps and I refuse. Not because I don't want them; I just need to get out of there. Angie makes me feel like a vampire caught in daylight.

I wait in the hallway while she goes to fetch Jay. I hear him complaining that he's in the middle of a game. Then he appears, sweaty and glaring. A couple of the other kids come out and stare at me until Angie shoos them away. Jay takes ages putting on his shoes, then finally we're back outside and I can breathe again.

"Harry thinks you're weird," Jay says, trailing behind me.

"Who's Harry? The little fat one?"

"Harry's not fat!"

"I'm not weird."

Jay's eyes flick to my ankles. "He says your trousers are too short."

"Maybe my legs are too long?"

Jay shoots me a look of contempt but doesn't say anything.

Harry's right, though—my trousers are too short, but that's the least of my worries. I'm thinking about what

Buchan said, and wondering what Han is up to in town while I'm stuck here, babysitting my miserable little brother.

I'm listening to Baz on the radio in the kitchen. It's nearly time for the quiz to start. I need to go down to the phone box, but Mum's not back yet. She should have been home ages ago. On a Wednesday, she finishes work at seven, so even if she stops at the off-licence on the way home, she's always back by quarter past.

I'll have to take Jay down with me. I can't risk leaving him here. If Mum comes back and finds him on his own, she'll go ballistic. She's probably staying on late at the chippy to help Mrs. Choi, so there's a chance she might see us in the phone box. It's a risk I'll have to take. If I don't phone the radio station in time, I'll be disqualified.

I leave Mum a note on the kitchen table, telling her I've taken Jay to the park. I'll probably get it in the ear for keeping him out late, but I can cope with that.

"You've got to be quiet," I tell Jay as we squeeze into the phone box.

He pulls a face. "It smells funny."

"I know. Don't worry about it."

"Why are we here?"

"I told you—I need to make a phone call."

"Who to?"

"Somebody from school—a friend. It's about some homework. Be quiet."

Jay sticks out his tongue as I dial the number.

"Radio Ham," says a voice in my ear.

"Hello. It's Daniel Roach for *Baz's Bedtime Bonanza.*"

"Hi, Mr. Roach, are you on the usual number? I'll get Cheryl to call you back."

"Thanks." I put the receiver back onto the cradle.

Jay is frowning at me. "You're not Daniel Roach. You're Laurence Roach. Why did you tell them that?"

"It's a code. We have special names for each other. Just a game, really."

"Oh," says Jay. "Me and Matt do that. I'm Growl and he's Wild Beast, but if Billy plays then he has to be Wild Beast and Matt is Swift, but Billy normally plays football, so Matt can be Wild Beast, and sometimes, if I feel like it, I'm Swift…"

The phone rings.

"Hi, Daniel. Cheryl here."

"Hi, Cheryl," I say, doing my Mr. Buchan impression.

"How are you this evening?"

"Yeah, fine thanks."

"Good stuff. Almost halfway there—you're doing really well."

"Thanks."

"We're going straight to the quiz when this record finishes—in about two minutes. So when you hear Baz talking that means you're on air. OK? Good luck!"

"Thanks."

"Why are you talking funny?" says Jay, looking up at me with his arms folded.

"We do voices too. Now you have to be quiet."

Jay frowns. "Why do I have to be quiet? It's not up to you anyway."

"Please, Jay! Just for a few minutes. I have to concentrate."

Jay pulls a face, then turns his back on me as the record fades...

"The HOUR strikes nine!" says Baz, his voice booming in my ear. "Which means it's TIME! For the BIG—BAZ—*Bedtime Bonanza*!" The sound of klaxons and wild cheering fills the studio. "Please welcome back—for his FOURTH day in the game—our REIGNING CHAMPION—MR. DANIEL—DANNY BOY—ROACHAAAA! How you doing, champ?"

"OK."

Baz laughs. "That's what I LOVE about you, my friend. Nothing fazes you. COOL as ice! Even though you are now just seven days—count them, boys and girls—just SEVEN DAYS away from WINNING an all-expenses-paid trip of a LIFETIME, courtesy of our very good friends at Hardacre Holidaze!" *Cue jingle.* "So Daniel, I've got to ask—do you feel lucky?"

Jay presses his lips against the wall of the kiosk and licks the glass. I pull him away.

"Get off!" He glares at me.

"Whoa!" says Baz, in my ear. "Are you all right there, champ?"

"Yeah, fine, sorry!" Too late, I realize I forgot to do the accent. I just spoke to Baz in my normal voice!

34

"Sounds like you've got some HELP tonight," says Baz. Did he notice? He must have noticed!

"No! Er … just one of my lads."

"Ah!" says Baz. "And who might that be? INTRODUCE US!"

"Um, I've got James with me."

"HELLO, JAMES!" says Baz. "And how old is he, Daniel?"

"Six."

"I'm not your lad!" says Jay.

"What's that?" Baz chuckles. "Hey, put him on, Dan, let's SPEAK to him."

My heart thumps a warning. The last thing I want is Jay live on the radio. "Er … I dunno, he's a bit shy."

"I'm not shy!" says Jay, very loudly.

"Yeah, I'm feeling lucky tonight, Baz," I say quickly, trying to change the subject. I glare at Jay and put a finger over my lips.

"Glad to hear it, my friend," says Baz. "Glad to HEAR IT. Let's hope young James will be a lucky mascot for you tonight."

"Yeah," I say as Jay sinks his teeth into my leg and starts to chew. At least with a mouthful of my jeans he can't make too much noise.

We get back to the flat, and there's nobody waiting for us except the roaches. I crumple up my note and bury it in the bin, then tell Jay it's time for bed.

"Not going to bed."

"Yes, you are."

"It's not up to you!"

"Mum's not here, so it is up to me, actually."

Jay's face twitches while he tries to think of a reply. "I'll tell Mum you made me go to the telephone with you."

"So?" I hadn't thought about that, but it doesn't matter. I'll say I had to phone Han about some homework. Mum hardly listens to what Jay tells her anyway.

Jay growls and drops to all fours, then advances towards me, snapping his teeth. I wonder if all six-year-old kids are like this, or is it just me who's got a lunatic for a brother?

At least I got through tonight, no thanks to Jay. The questions were easy—three out of three again. Only six more days to go. Just eighteen questions. I'm starting to believe I might actually win.

I imagine Mum's face when I present her with the holiday … *She's just back from the chippy, sitting at the kitchen table, cigarette in one hand, glass of wine in the other, with that dead look in her eyes. I give her the envelope and she stares at it, frowning. She probably thinks it's a letter from school, telling her I've been expelled or something—until she sees the Hardacre Holidaze packet inside.*

Mum leans forward and rests her ciggie on the ashtray so she can use both hands, because she's interested now. She pulls out the tickets and the brochure showing us where we're going, then looks at me. The dead glaze has gone from her eyes.

Her whole face is changing. It's as if the person she was—

the one I remember from years ago—is coming back. She's
smiling and there are tears rolling down her cheeks, but they're
happy tears. They make her eyes sparkle.

I do my homework, then make myself a coffee and go into
the front room. Jay's asleep on the settee. I switch off the TV
and carry him to bed. He squirms and mutters something
about Wild Beast, but he's not really awake. The Scooby-Doo
alarm clock says 10:37 p.m.

Mum must have got paid tonight and gone to the pub.
She'll come crashing in around midnight and fall asleep on
the settee, which means I'll have to do her cleaning shift in
the morning.

That reminds me what Mr. Buchan said: if I'm late three
more times, they'll put me on report. Mum won't like that.

I touch the tender area around my eye. Somehow I need
to start getting to registration on time. I wonder, could I have
invisibility *and* super speed? That might do it.

I lie in the dark, listening—waiting for Mum to come home.
It's midnight and I'm wide awake. In five hours' time the
alarm will go off.

In some countries they use sleep deprivation as a form
of torture.

BLURSDAY

I turn off the alarm before it starts. I've been awake for hours, drifting between sleep and consciousness, listening for Mum.

The light in the hall scratches at my eyes as I stumble across to her room. I stand in the doorway for a moment, blinking at the empty bed, then check the front room. She's not in there either, but I'm not really surprised—it's not the first time Mum's stayed out all night.

I should go and do her shift, but I can't leave Jay on his own in the flat. If Mum comes back and I haven't gone to work, she'll go mad. But if she comes back and finds Jay here on his own, she'll go mad about that too.

Maybe she already left and I didn't hear her?

But her cleaning overall is still here, hanging over a chair in the bedroom.

Unless she went straight there from wherever she spent the night. She might have the key card with her. That makes sense.

I don't bother to check her overall pocket, the one where she always keeps the card. I just go back to bed.

The sound of the television wakes me. Jay's bed is empty

and light is pumping through the window. The numbers on the Scooby-Doo clock tell me we're late.

In the front room, Jay's lying upside down on the settee in his pajamas. I switch off the TV and tell him to get dressed.

"I'm hungry."

"We're late."

"I want some breakfast!" He gets up and switches the television back on.

"Jay! We haven't got time!" I know already there's no way I'll make it today. Another strike on Mr. Buchan's list.

I switch off the television again and grab Jay as he tries to turn it back on.

"Go and get dressed!"

"I want to watch TV!" He swings a fist at me.

"No hitting! What does Mum say about hitting?"

"She does it to you!" Jay glares at me.

"Go and get dressed and I'll make you some toast."

"Don't want toast!"

"It's all we've got."

"I hate toast!" screams Jay, and then he stamps off towards the bedroom.

The bread's gone hard, but I can't see any green bits. I put two slices in the toaster, then go to the bedroom where Jay is throwing clothes around. I forgot to go to the launderette last night; my school shirts are still in a dirty pile on the floor. All I can do is pick one and coat the thing in deodorant. The sticky cloth clings to me like a rash.

I smell the toast burning a second before the smoke alarm goes off.

"She's hot, man!" Han shows me the picture on his phone again. The girl's face is too blurred to see it properly, but I nod anyway.

"Nice."

"Nice? Man!" Han gazes at the screen. "You should've come up the Arcade last night—she's got friends!" His eyebrows do a Mexican wave. "I'm meeting them Sunday, yeah—at the festival. You gotta be there, man."

"What festival?"

"In the park, Sunday. Loads of bands and stuff. It's all sorted, I tell you!"

"If I can, yeah." If Mum's in a good mood—if it's safe to leave Jay on his own with her—I might be able to get out for a while.

Han puts his mobile back into his pocket. "You coming for a game? Mike's got his footy with him."

I shake my head. "I've got some homework to finish."

Han shrugs. "OK. Later, man!"

The library is in the old part of the school, a long narrow room with high ceilings and tall sash windows. It smells damp and musty, even on days like today. I walk between the shadowy bookshelves to the Media Center—a grand name for a few tables and a row of computers at the far end of the room. It's virtually deserted, which suits me.

I was lying about the homework, but I have got things to do. I've been thinking about what Baz said the other night, about a sport question—it made me realize I know nothing about sport. I haven't bothered to study before, but now I'm starting to believe I might actually win. I want to give myself a chance. It can't hurt, can it?

I choose a terminal and log on to the system, then enter *sporting facts* into a search engine. A page of links pops up: *Interesting Facts: Sports and Games, 10 Sports Trivia Facts, Freaky Sports Facts.* I try the first one, but it's all old stuff about the original Olympic Games in 776 BC and how the Ancient Romans played a game a bit like golf, using sticks and a leather ball stuffed with feathers. I can't imagine Baz asking me anything like that. The next site is American— loads of stuff about baseball and why American footballers put black stuff under their eyes.

I try another search. This time I type *Sports Quiz Questions* and add *UK* to the end. The first website brings up a page of questions: *In snooker, how many red balls are on the table at the start of a game? Which sport uses different colored balls depending on temperature? On a dart board, what number is directly opposite number one?* There's a button at the end of each line to find out the answer. I don't know any of them. Perhaps I should write some down? I could try to memorize a few for tonight. But there are three screens of questions; it will take ages.

The more I read, the more panic crowds in on me. Baz might ask me any of these questions, or a million others. I could spend the rest of the day looking through this stuff and still know next to nothing. Maybe it's better to leave it? Trust in fate. It's worked so far.

"Stupid thing!"

The voice comes from close by. A girl is standing over the printer table, swearing. She snatches a sheet of paper as it rolls into the tray and growls, then moves to a computer and starts hitting keys. Each thump is accompanied by a different oath. I'm impressed. Most people can swear, but for variety and invention, this girl is a master.

"Are you going to help or just sit there gawping?" She turns and glares at me.

"What?"

She points at the computer. "This thing won't do what I tell it!" Her accent sounds funny, northern.

"What's wrong with it?" I stand up. It looks like I'm helping whether I want to or not.

"I'm trying to print these out." The girl waves the scrunched-up sheets of paper at me. "But it keeps coming out the wrong size."

"How big do you want it?"

"I want it to fit on here, don't I?" She looks at me like I'm an idiot.

I sit down at the terminal. I'm no techno geek—we've never had a computer at home—but I've learned the quirks of the school printers.

"You have to choose this tray. Look." I point to the screen. "And select *fit to printable area*."

"I did that!"

I shrug as the printer groans into life and grinds out another page.

"Yes!" The girl grabs the sheet and punches the air in triumph. "You're a genius!" She grins. "Right—I want twenty."

We wait while the printer chugs out another twenty copies. I can feel her watching me.

"What you doing in here anyway?" she says after a moment. "Shouldn't you be out on the field playing footy with your mates?"

"I don't really like football."

"Really? I thought that was all lads ever talk about. Lucky for me, eh?"

I look at her and swallow.

"I mean, there's never normally a geek around when you need one."

"I'm not a geek!"

She laughs. "Just playing with you, Big Man! No offence intended. Anyway, wouldn't matter to me if you were. I quite like geeks."

I turn away and pick up one of the sheets coming off the printer, hoping my cheeks aren't as red as they feel. "Um … so what's this for anyway?"

It says *Pop in the Park* across the top of the poster. I realize it must be the thing Han was going on about—Hardacre's very own summer music festival. There's a list of local bands I haven't heard of, but the headline act—the big finale before the fireworks—is a Queen tribute band. Mum would like that. Maybe we could all go? If she's in a good mood.

"Can I keep this?"

The girl frowns. "I suppose, seeing as how you helped. You going to come?"

"Might do."

She points to one of the names halfway down the list. "That's me. Brass-O!"

"You're in a band?" I'm surprised. She doesn't look the type. "What do you play?"

"Trumpet … it's a brass band. Brass-O! D'you get it? Like *Hawaii Five-O*, but with brass—like the polish. We play that—the *Hawaii Five-O* theme song."

"Great."

"It's lame!" She shrugs. "But I don't have much choice. My dad's the band leader. Been doing it since I was five."

"Yeah?"

She collects her posters together. "Right, better get these up before the bell goes. Thanks for your help—you're my hero!"

"No problem." I get the feeling she's being sarcastic.

"I'm Mina, by the way," she says, picking up her bag. "What are they going to carve on your gravestone?"

"What?"

"Or did they only give you a number?"

"Eh?"

"What's your *name*, Big Man?" She sighs and shakes her head. "I sometimes think you lot speak a different language down here."

"Oh, right … Laurence. Laurence Roach."

"Pleased to meet you, Laurence Laurence Roach. See you on Sunday then."

The way Mina talks, it's more of a command than an invitation.

Nelly's at her post when we get home.

"Hello, boys!"

I grunt.

"How's your mother? Is she not well?"

"She's fine."

"Only I've not seen her today."

I don't look at her, afraid my face will give me away. I wonder if she knows Mum didn't come home last night.

"Had a bit of a fire this morning did we?"

"What?"

"I heard your smoke alarm go off!"

"It wasn't a fire, just the toast."

"That was fortunate." Nelly's eyes lock on to mine like a homing missile. "It would be a tragedy if anything happened while you were there all on your own."

"We're not." I look back at her, straight down the barrel. "Come on, Jay, let's go and see Mum."

I can feel Nelly tracking us, all the way up the stairs.

"Mum!" calls Jay, running ahead. "Mum?" He goes in and out of all the rooms, then turns on me. "You said Mum was here!"

I shrug and dump my bag in the hall. "I said that to shut Nosy Nelly up."

Jay growls, then storms into the front room and slams the door.

I check the flat. Nothing has changed. Mum hasn't been home.

She must have found somebody to get drunk with last night and crashed out somewhere after the pub. She probably slept all day, then woke up just in time to do her shift at the chippy. There's nothing to worry about. She'll be home later, bad tempered and hung over, and everything will be back to normal.

I go into the kitchen to do my homework; I don't want any more grief from school.

There's a cockroach on the wall by the cooker. Sitting there with its antennae quivering. It's giving me the creeps. I can feel goose bumps crawling across my skin just looking at it.

I stand quietly and pick up a frying pan from the sink.

The roach doesn't move.

I take a step closer.

The weapon feels good and heavy in my hand.

I take aim ... and let him have it—

The noise as the pan hits the wall is immense. My ears are still ringing as I check underneath for roach remains. But instead of guts all over the wall, there's just a greasy smear and a dent in the plaster.

"What are you doing?"

I turn round. Jay is watching me from the doorway.

"Chasing roaches," I tell him.

"Did you get it?"

"No."

He shakes his head. "You can't kill them, you know."

"What?"

"A cockroach doesn't die even if you chop its head off."

"Don't talk rubbish!"

Jay frowns. "It's not rubbish! We learnt it at school. Miss Shaw said a cockroach can live for days without its head!"

"What about if you squash it with a frying pan?"

"Dunno." He shrugs. "We didn't talk about that."

I put the pan back in the sink.

"I'm hungry," says Jay. "Where's Mum?"

"At work," I tell him, dropping the last crust of stale bread into the toaster.

"I don't want toast!"

"It's all we've got."

His eyes darken. "I want Mum to come home. You're rubbish." Jay stomps back into the other room and slams the door.

"Fine, I'll eat the toast then. Let him starve," I tell the roaches, while I look in the cupboard for some jam.

The smoke alarm makes me jump. I stand on a chair to pull the battery out and imagine Nelly in the flat below, making a note in her surveillance log. Something else for her to complain about.

I tell Jay I'll buy him a present if he's quiet while I'm on the phone.

He doesn't want to come into the kiosk with me, though. "It smells of wee in there."

"OK, you can wait outside, but you have to stay there, next to the phone box. Don't go running off!"

Jay looks at me. "It's not up to you!"

"If you don't stay here and keep quiet, I'm not buying you anything."

He scowls and leans back against the phone box, pulling his cap down over his eyes.

I'm nervous tonight. More nervous than before. I can't stop thinking about all those sports questions, page after page rolling across the screen—there's so much I don't know.

Baz will ask me a sport question tonight. I can feel it.

"Two down, just ONE TO GO!" says Baz, followed by a fanfare of trumpets.

There's somebody outside waiting to use the telephone, and Jay's pulling faces at me through the glass. I try to ignore them both and concentrate on what Baz is saying. So far I've been lucky—and no sport.

"QUESTION number three!" says Baz. "What did Florence Nightingale carry in her pocket wherever she went? Was it A: a stethoscope? B: a lamp? Or C: an owl? I'll read that again for you…"

That's easy. Florence Nightingale was *the Lady with the Lamp*. Everybody knows that.

"A lamp," I tell Baz. "B."

The line goes silent.

"Daniel," says Baz, very quiet and calm. He always does

this voice, like he's about to give me bad news, just before he tells me I'm right and I'm through to the next round.

But not this time.

"That's the WRONG answer."

My heart drops to the bottom of my rib cage and rolls around like a lost football.

"Florence Nightingale," says Baz, "actually carried a baby OWL in her pocket! Which MEANS—it's time to bring in our CHALLENGER! Who's on line two tonight, Cheryl?"

"Hello?" A woman's voice. She sounds nervous.

"Aha! A LADY challenger! Excellent! And who might you be, my love?"

"Hello, Baz, it's Shirley . . . Shirley Powers, from Marston."

"SHIRLEEE POWERS! WELCOME to the show, Shirley. That's a great name, POWERS! Are you Mrs. Powers? Did you ACQUIRE that name? Or have you always been powerful?"

Shirley laughs. "It's my husband's name."

"Well, it's YOUR name as well now!" says Baz. "So, Shirley—are you feeling powerful tonight? Have you got the POWER to challenge our champion?"

"Yep. Sure have, Baz," says Shirley, sounding more confident every minute.

"FANTASTIC!" says Baz. "That's what I LIKE to hear! But more importantly—DO YOU FEEL LUCKEEE?"

Shirley feels lucky.

I don't, and I'm getting daggers from the bloke waiting to use the phone. He's wearing a *Bartman—Avenger of Evil* T-shirt, with a picture of Bart Simpson in superhero guise—

except the picture's all warped and distorted by the gigan-
tic belly underneath. I've never seen anyone look *less* like an
avenger of evil than this guy.

Shirley's first question is a sport one. I don't know the
answer, but she does. Straight away, no problem. Lucky? She
just knows.

Question two: music. How easy are they going to make
it? I bet Baz chooses the questions deliberately. All these
things are fixed. They don't want anyone to actually win!

The bloke outside bangs on the wall of the phone box
and shouts through the glass. "Are you going to be long?"

I shake my head and make apologetic shrugging gestures. He scowls and looks at his watch. Jay has stopped pulling faces at me and is watching Bartman instead, but I'm not
really concentrating on them. Something marvellous has just
happened—Shirley got her question wrong! Which means
I'm still in with a chance.

"THIS is what it's all about, boys and girls!" says Baz.
"Two MIGHTY warriors locked HEAD TO HEAD in mor-
tal combat! OK, maybe not mortal—but HEY! This is *Baz's
Bedtime Bonanza*! This ain't playtime!" The theme music from
the *Rocky* films starts playing in the background. "So this is
where we are, folks. In the BLUE corner—Daniel THE ICE-
MAN Roach, with TWO correct answers on the board. In the
RED corner, our challenger this evening—Shirley SUPER
Powers, our very own Wonder Woman! Shirley has one answer
on the board, one miss, and ONE MORE CHANCE to take
Danny Boy, our reigning *Baz's Bedtime Bonanza* champion,
to a SUDDEN-DEATH knock-out! But..." Baz pauses and

the line hums. "If Shirley gets this one wrong—then Daniel is through to the next round. It's down to you, Shirley. Have YOU got THE POWER? Are you READY?"

"Ready," says Shirley, still sounding confident.

"Do you FEEL lucky?"

I don't catch Shirley's answer because there's a noise outside—a strange high-pitched yelp.

I look through the glass and see Jay hanging from Bartman's trouser leg by his teeth. I can only guess that the bloke was about to hassle me again and Jay slipped into Attack Dog mode.

I clamp my hand over the mouthpiece of the telephone and push open the door.

"Jay! What are you doing?"

Jay looks at me and lets go.

"What's wrong with him?" says Bartman, backing away.

"I'm sorry."

"Sorry? He should be locked up. He's not right in the head!"

Jay growls and lunges for him again. The Avenger of Evil almost trips in his haste to get away.

"Jay! Leave! Come here, good boy!" I say, slapping my thigh. It sounds crazy, but it's the only thing Jay will respond to when he's in this mood.

The bloke stares at us. "You're mad, both of you. I should call the police!"

For a second I panic—that's the last thing we need! Then I remember what I'm holding.

"Maybe you should," I say, waving the telephone at him. "Too bad the phone's in use!"

I grab Jay and pull him inside the kiosk with me, then put the receiver back to my ear. I hope they didn't catch any of that on air.

The line is dead.

No!

Does that mean I lost? Did they cut me off because I'm out?

But if Shirley got her question right, it would mean a sudden-death knock-out...

Frantically, I dial the radio station again. It rings for ages before somebody answers.

"Good evening, Radio Ham!"

"Hello, it's Daniel Roach. I think I got cut off."

"I beg your pardon?"

"It's Daniel Roach. I was on *Baz's Bedtime Bonanza*— the quiz."

"I'm afraid you're too late. It's already started."

"No! I know! I was on it. I got cut off!"

"I'm sorry, sir, you're too late." I realize it's a different voice than the one who normally answers. This person doesn't know who I am!

"Please! They need me for the knock-out! I got cut off! Ask Cheryl—Baz's producer. Tell her it's Daniel Roach. Please!"

The woman lets out a long sigh, just so I know exactly how much of her time I'm wasting. "Hold the line."

The phone clicks and Baz's voice is in my ear... *Daniel, are you there?*

"Yeah, I'm here!"

We seem to have lost Daniel, says Baz. *Has Mr. Ice finally CRACKED under the pressure?*

"No! I'm here!" I'm screaming down the phone, but Baz can't hear me!

Now he's talking about Pop in the Park... *we'll have LOADS of Radio Ham goodies to give away: T-shirts, hats, badges—and I'll be doing a SPECIAL one-off, Baz in the Park Bonanza, with a MEGA mind-blowing prize for the winner! You'd be a MONKEY to miss it!*

Then a record comes on and I realize what's happening. When you phone up Radio Ham and they put you on hold, they play what's going out on-air to you on the phone. Baz isn't talking to me; he's on the radio. But what happened in the quiz? What did he mean about me cracking under the pressure?

There's a click and the woman comes back on the line.

"I'll just put you through, sir."

"Hi, Daniel!" I've never been so glad to hear Cheryl's voice. "We lost you. I'm not quite sure what happened."

"I dunno, the line just went dead." I wonder how much she heard.

"Not to worry. I don't know when you were disconnected, but you'll be pleased to hear that Shirley got her third question wrong, so you're through to the next round."

I stagger from the phone box dripping with sweat.

Thankfully there's no sign of Bartman. All the same, it might be wise to make ourselves scarce in case he comes back.

"Why did you bite that man?"

"I didn't," says Jay. "*I* told him to be quiet because you needed to concentrate on the telephone, but he wouldn't listen. So I turned into Scooby-Doo, and *he* bit him."

I nod. "Right … OK." I ruffle Jay's hair. "Good dog!"

"*I'm* not a dog, stupid!"

"Sorry! Well … tell Scooby I said thanks, next time you see him then."

"OK," says Jay.

For the second time in two nights, I go into the kitchen and throw away the note I left for Mum.

Where is she? She should be back by now. What if something *has* happened to her?

The thought rests an icy hand on my neck.

I shrug it off and remind myself that it wouldn't be the first time she's left us on our own for a few days. Besides, if something bad had happened, an accident or something, the police would have been round here by now.

Mum'll be fine—it's me and Jay I need to worry about. I learned *that* lesson the hard way.

A year before we moved here, Mum tried to kill herself.

I got back from school and I knew something was wrong the moment I opened the door. The television was on, but the front room was empty. I called out, but nobody answered. I assumed they'd gone out until I saw the spilled drink on the carpet and biscuits all over the settee. Mum would never have left a mess like that, not in those days.

I tried the kitchen and checked the garden, then went upstairs. The bedroom I shared with Jay was empty; so was the bathroom. I left Mum's room till last.

The curtains were closed. It was dark and shadowy inside, but I could see them both lying on the bed. For a moment I thought they were dead. I couldn't move—just stood there in the doorway thinking I was going to be sick. Then Jay's head shot up and he grinned at me.

"Didn't you hear me calling?" I was angry and relieved at the same time.

Jay just laughed and said "Boo!" like it was a game. Then I realized Mum still hadn't moved.

"Mum asleep!" said Jay, giving her a prod. "She's been asleep ages! I'm bored." He climbed off the bed. "Come and play with me."

I was sure she was dead then.

I took Jay downstairs and told him to watch some telly. I didn't want to go back up, but I had to.

The room smelt bad. I made myself switch on the light, and that's when I saw the sick on the carpet, a trail of it from Mum's mouth across the duvet. Her eyes were closed and her skin was the color of Blu-Tack, but she was still breathing.

I ran straight out of the house and got Sheila from next door. That was my first mistake. But I didn't know any better then; I still trusted people. I'd always been told that if I ever needed help, I was to go and find a policeman or tell a grown-up and they would know what to do.

The ambulance came and took Mum away, and me and Jay had to go and stay next door with Sheila and Graeme. Sheila was nice—she used to come round and drink coffee with Mum sometimes—but I didn't really know Graeme. I got the feeling he didn't want us there. So when it was Jay's bedtime I volunteered to go up as well, just to get out of Graeme's way.

We were sharing a big double bed and I think I must have fallen asleep, because Jay woke me up, snivelling. At first I thought he was just missing Mum, but then I felt the wet on his pajamas and saw the stain on the sheets. They probably wouldn't have found out, except Sheila chose that exact moment to come and check that we were all right.

She was fine about it, though, and started to get clean sheets out of a cupboard, but then Graeme came in. He saw what had happened and went ballistic. Jay started crying and Graeme shouted at him to shut up. When Jay didn't stop, Graeme slapped him.

For a second nobody moved. It was like in a film when the action freezes and the camera pans round so you can see everyone's face. Graeme was at the opposite side of the bed, leaning over Jay, the veins in his neck bulging. The next thing I knew, I was flying through the air towards him. I think the surprise knocked him off balance, because we both ended up in a heap on the floor—which is when I started laying into him until Sheila dragged me off.

After that, I had to go and stay with a kid I knew from

school, leaving Jay with Sheila and Graeme. I was allowed to go round and see him each evening, before Graeme got home from work, but when it was time for me to leave, Jay always got really upset. It was horrible. I used to lie awake thinking about him, just a few streets away, all by himself.

There was nothing I could do about it. I tried telling people what had happened, but nobody would listen. They even sent me to a doctor who said I was *transferring the grief and anger of Mum trying to commit suicide* onto Graeme.

My Nanna used to say that a mistake didn't have to be a mistake—not if you learned from it. So I made myself a promise. Next time, if there was a next time, I wouldn't make the same mistakes. Next time, *I* would decide what was best for me and Jay—and nobody was going to split us up again.

Which means I can't let anybody know that Mum's not here—not even Jay. I don't trust him to keep his mouth shut. I'll tell him she's doing extra shifts at work or something. Until she comes back, we have to carry on like normal and make everyone think that Mum is still here.

How hard can it be?

LIEDAY

I find the wig in a plastic bag at the bottom of Mum's wardrobe. Thick, chestnut red, and curly. I remember the morning I came down to breakfast and discovered that Mum had shaved all her hair off. She cried for two whole days, then went out and bought the wig. It was almost exactly the same as her real hair, and she wore it all the time for about six months, until her hair grew back.

I pull it on now, tucking my own dull brown curls under the itchy cap, but I still look nothing like her. Maybe some lipstick would help? I sift through the tubes on Mum's dressing table and pick one called Vampire's Kiss. It tastes funny and I get loads on my teeth. I frown into the gloom of Mum's mirror at the boy with the blood-smeared lips and curly red wig. This is never going to work.

But I have to try. I have to make everything look normal—the same as always. And every morning Nelly watches Mum leave the building on her way to work—except yesterday. If Nelly doesn't see Mum today, she's going to get even more suspicious.

I pick up Mum's cleaning overall and put it on, then look back at the figure reflected in the mirror.

I wonder—will Nelly see Mum? Or me, dressed up like a pantomime dame?

I wedge the bedroom window open and check that Jay is still asleep, then walk down the hall and out of the flat before I can change my mind. I close the door quietly, then remember that Mum always slams it—but I can't risk waking Jay. Besides, I'm terrified somebody is going to come out of one of the other flats. But it's six in the morning—the only person likely to be up is Nosy Nelly, and that's the whole point. I wonder why she bothers, though. I mean, what's she got to get up for? All she does is sit in her flat all day, spying on people. She never goes out anywhere, and she's got no friends that I've ever seen. Maybe that's why she's so miserable.

Down the stairs and through the door into the lobby. I let this one bang behind me, and the noise booms off the walls like a football in a dustbin. The tiles on the floor hum with an orange glow from the streetlamp outside. I focus on the exit, forcing myself not to look as I walk past Nelly's flat. I make a bet: if I can hold my breath until I get outside, then this is going to work.

My head feels like a balloon; I can hear blood pumping through my ears with each footstep. When I reach the front door, I pull instead of push and have to press the release button again. Finally I'm outside, gulping in the cool early morning air. I walk down the steps, careful to keep my face turned away from the windows of Nelly's flat. I can feel her watching me all the way.

But who is she seeing?

Me, or Mum?

I go as far as the end of the street, then double back, ducking down the service road behind the shops. Nelly mustn't see me going back in, so I use the fire escape. I've got one leg through the bedroom window when I notice Jay, sitting up in bed, staring at me.

"What you doing?"

For a second I freeze, straddling the windowsill. Then I see his eyes and realize he's still asleep. Jay does this a lot, usually in the middle of the night. You can have a whole conversation with him and he won't remember anything about it in the morning.

I close the window and go over to his bed. He looks at me and frowns, and I remember I'm still dressed up like Mum.

"It's not time to get up yet," I tell him, trying to make my voice sound like hers.

Jay shivers for a moment, then lies back down and screws his eyes shut. I kneel next to the bed and stroke his hair, and after a few minutes his breathing is steady. I stand up quietly and slip out of the room.

It's still early, but my brain is buzzing too much to go back to bed. I get dressed for school, then switch on the TV. There's nothing much on, so I watch three episodes of *Pingu*, then fall asleep. When I wake up, Jay is sitting next to me.

I tell him that Mum came back late last night and now she's gone to work. I don't want him to tell anyone that she's not here.

"I know," he says. "I saw her."

"What?" Something kicks me in the chest from the inside.

"I saw her before she went," says Jay. "You were still asleep."

My mind spools—did Mum come back while I was asleep here? Or earlier, before I went out?

"She was in our room," he says. "Sitting in the window."

Then I realize he's talking about me.

I breathe out and allow myself a grin. It looks like my Dawn Deception might have worked better than I expected. I just hope Nosy Nelly was as easily fooled.

After school the House of Fun is strangely quiet.

"They're just watching the end of..." Angie frowns at the DVD case. "*Alien Space Monkey Pirates II.*" She pulls a face. "I don't normally encourage television, but Robert brought it round especially, so I couldn't really say no."

A burst of the *Alien Space Monkey Pirates* theme floats from the living room, and suddenly I'm nine again—I can taste ice cream on my tongue and hear Mum laughing in the seat beside me.

She took me to see *Alien Space Monkey Pirates*, the first film, as a special treat. We went to the big multiplex cinema in town. I'd never seen anything like it. They had the names of the films in lights over the doors, and inside, next to the ticket booths, giant cardboard cut-outs of the characters. I liked the one called Grissom best. He didn't say much, but he was tough and brave—always there to get the others out of trouble.

I got a Grissom action figure for Christmas that year, a present from Greg—when he was still just Mum's boyfriend, before he became Jay's dad. I liked Greg then—he was good fun and Mum was happy. But when he left and Mum got depressed and started drinking again, I blamed him. I hated him for abandoning us. And every time I played with Grissom, I remembered that Greg had bought him for me, so I started to hate Grissom too.

So I killed him.

Grissom—not Greg.

I pretended he was on a daring mission that went wrong—and threw him out of my bedroom window. He landed in the road outside our house and just lay there looking up at me. A car came and ran over him, but he didn't break. I felt really bad because I didn't hate Grissom; I loved him. But I felt so angry at Greg, I had to do something, destroy something—even if it made me feel bad. I could have gone down and fetched Grissom back, but I didn't. I made myself stay there and watch as more cars came and then a truck, and when the truck passed over, Grissom was gone, just like that.

I cried then, even though it was only a toy. Because it felt like something *had* died, like a big hole had opened up inside me, a hole I didn't know how to close up again.

"Are you all right, love?" Angie is frowning at me, her head tilted to one side.

"Yeah … I'm fine."

"I don't know how much longer there is to go … but you might as well have a drink." She thrusts a glass of milk into my hand before I can refuse. "Mum OK?"

I almost choke. "Fine, yeah."

"Jolly good! I only ask because she normally comes on a Friday … to settle up for the week." Angie punctuates the sentence with a little cough and I feel like the floor has just vanished from beneath me.

The money!

I forgot about the money!

"Mum didn't give me the envelope. Sorry! She's … she couldn't come today."

I'm starting to sweat—I'm a vampire again, Angie advancing towards me with a wooden stake in her hand.

"She must have forgotten—I'll bring it round tomorrow." I shrug.

Sometimes a shrug just fits. Sometimes you can get away with stuff, when you're a fifteen-year-old boy, if you just pretend you're useless. Angie expects me to be clueless, so I don't disappoint her, and I get away with it—for now.

"Oh, don't worry!" Angie waves her hands. "No rush, you can bring it next week."

Next week.

Mum will be back by then, so there's nothing to worry about.

Jay tells me the entire story of *Alien Space Monkey Pirates II* on the way home. He's impressed by how much I know about them and can't believe they existed when I was small. I tell Jay about my Grissom, but not what happened to him.

We stop at the newsagent's in the Parade and I buy Jay the Pokémon cards I promised him.

"Are we going to the phone box again tonight?" he asks, eyeing the box of trading cards.

"Probably."

"Do you want me to be quiet again?"

I sigh and dig into my pocket for another coin. It's the last of the change from Mum's dressing table. I hope there's some more money back at the flat. We need to buy something proper to eat. Jay will throw a fit if I try to give him toast again tonight.

The china piggybank feels reassuringly heavy when I get it down from on top of the fridge. I pry the rubber plug from its belly and spill the contents onto the kitchen table.

"Wow!" says Jay. "We're rich!"

"Not exactly." Mum puts all her loose change in here, so it's mostly copper, but there are a few bits of silver: tens, twenties, even a fifty. I spread the pile with my hand.

"You want to help me count it?"

"OK," says Jay, then he frowns. "This is Mum's money— not yours!"

"It's OK. She said we could use some. To buy something to eat. She said she might be working late again tonight. So we've got to have dinner on our own."

I let Jay make towers with the copper while I count the silver.

"Why does Mum put her money in a pig?" Jay half closes one eye and balances another penny onto an already precarious stack.

"Nanna used to collect them. D'you remember Nanna?"

Jay screws up his face, then shakes his head.

"She had loads of them, all different colors, on shelves in her kitchen. She used to let you play with them when you were little."

Jay stops what he's doing and looks at me. "Where are they now?"

"Well...when Nanna died, Mum brought them to our house."

"Really?" For a moment his face brightens, then he frowns. "No she didn't. I haven't seen any pigs. Where are they?"

"We haven't got them anymore. Just this one."

"Where did they go?"

"I don't know. Mum got rid of them, I think."

I don't tell him about the night I woke up and thought someone was breaking into the house. How I lay there holding my breath, too scared to move, listening to the crashing and banging downstairs—and then the other noise. It took me ages to realize what it was, because burglars don't usually start crying in the middle of a robbery.

I don't tell Jay how I crept halfway down the stairs until I could see Mum, on her hands and knees in the front room, surrounded by a sea of smashed china pigs. I knew she'd done it, but I didn't know why, and I was afraid to go down.

Next morning I found her sitting at the kitchen table. She looked pale and tired, and her eyes were red from crying. There were white bandages around her hands and both wrists, and the table was covered with bits of broken pig. She was trying to glue them back together.

"Look what I did to Nanna's pigs," she said, trying to smile.

I didn't know what to say, so I looked at the pieces of china on the table. There were some quite big bits—complete heads with smiling faces, a rear end with a curly tail, or a leg sticking out of a curve of fat belly. When I looked back at Mum she was crying silently, her body shaking and tears streaming down her face.

Jay was playing on the floor, oblivious. I didn't know what to do. When I was little and I cried, Mum used to put me on her lap and give me a cuddle, and it made me feel better. That way round it made sense, but I couldn't put her on my lap, could I? I couldn't just walk over and put my arms round her. I was thirteen; it felt too weird.

I said I'd help her mend the pigs, because I didn't know what else to do. I couldn't just stand there gawping.

That made her cry even more, but at least she was smiling at the same time.

Out of all those pigs, and there must have been fifty or more, we only managed to put one back together. An ugly, cross-eyed blue thing with a pink-spotted bow-tie. We christened it Humpty.

I look at the pig now, sitting on the kitchen table, the glue running in ugly brown seams across its body—a Frankenstein's Monster of a piggy bank. Mum was so happy that we managed to put it back together. Of all the things she's sold or smashed since, she's never touched the pig.

There's more money in Humpty than I thought—over six pounds, and I haven't counted the copper yet. We go down to SavaShoppa in the Parade and buy bread, cereal, and milk for breakfast and a pizza for dinner. I'm so hungry I eat too much, too quickly. I spend the next half hour burping so loudly that Jay falls off the settee laughing.

It's past the hour that Mum should be home, but I hardly notice. Right now, I've got other things on my mind. I get the phonecards from under my mattress and tell Jay it's time to go.

"Sorry, Daniel my friend, but that's the WRONG answer!"

Not again! I'm struggling tonight. I've already had one lucky guess. Maybe this is it. I knew my luck would run out eventually. All I can do now is hope that tonight's challenger is rubbish and I get another chance.

Baz is introducing him...

"WHO have we got on line two?"

"All right, Baz, it's Mac here!"

"Mac?" says Baz. "Now, I'm no Sherlock Holmes, but would you by any chance be a SCOTSMAN?"

Mac chuckles. "Aye!"

"We're being INVADED!" says Baz. "TWO SCOTS-MEN—head to head! It's like that film—you know, the one with Sean Connery and the big sword—THERE CAN BE ONLY ONE!"

"*Highlander*," says Mac.

"That's it!"

The significance of this hits me like a bucket of iced water—just before Baz says, "Mac, meet Daniel Roach, your FELLOW COUNTRYMAN and our reigning *Baz's Bedtime Bonanza* champ!"

"All right, Dan," says Mac. "Where you from?"

My mouth goes dry, which is lucky because I think I was about to say *Scotland*. "Kilmarnock," I croak. "Like Johnnie Walker." My heart thunders in my ears. It's something Mr. Buchan said once. I haven't got a clue what it means. I don't know why I just said it.

"Ah right. I've got an uncle in Longpark."

"Yeah?" *Where's Longpark?*

"Where are YOU from, Mac?" says Baz.

"Glasgow."

"Ah!" says Baz. "Rangers or Celtic?"

"Rangers!"

"Are you a FOOTBALLING man, Daniel? Do you follow the MIGHTY Killie?"

Who?

"No, I'm not really into football."

"NOT into football? Are you SURE you're Scottish?"

What does he mean? Can he tell my accent is fake? Next

to the real thing, I sound as false as Baz doing his terrible *Highlander* impression.

"If I was from Killie, I wouldn't be into football either," says Mac, laughing.

"Ooh, now THERE's a gauntlet being slapped down if I ever heard one!" says Baz, cackling with delight. "Right, gentlemen, let the GAMES commence! And remember...THERE CAN BE ONLY ONE!"

Mac's questions are so easy Jay could answer them. They're doing this deliberately! I'm too close to winning—they want me off the show.

Then Mac gets one wrong. Which means a *Baz's Bedtime Bonanza* shoot-out.

Baz can hardly contain himself. "It's like TWO men in kilts standing atop a rugged hillside, WIELDING mighty claymores!" There's movie-soundtrack music playing in the background now; I'm guessing it's from *Highlander*.

"Gentlemen, let me remind you of the rules," says Baz. "As our reigning champion, Daniel goes first. If he answers correctly, he wins, simple as that. BUT...if Daniel gets it wrong...then Mac is in play. If Mac gets HIS question right—it's all over. There can BE only one...Gentlemen. SCOTSMEN! Are you ready? DO YOU FEEL LUCKY?"

"Yeah," I lie.

"Right," says Mac.

"Daniel," says Baz. "Which one of the following revolving weather systems is the smallest? Is it, A: typhoon? B: hurricane? Or C: tornado? I'll read that again..."

Baz can read it as many times as he likes; I don't know

the answer. I'm shivering and sweating at the same time. The phone box is full of my stink.

Think, Laurence. Concentrate.

Typhoon—that sounds big, but so does tornado. I don't know—hurricane? That doesn't sound so bad. But then ...

"Daniel," says Baz, "I need to push you for an answer."

I take a deep breath. "B: Hurricane." *It's a one-in-three chance. I could be lucky.*

A sound effect of clashing swords fills my ears, making me jump.

"There can be only one," says Baz in a strangely calm voice. "Daniel, my friend, I'm afraid a TORNADO is the smallest revolving weather system."

I've blown it. If Mac gets this one right, I'm out.

I lean my head against the cool glass of the phone box and watch Jay attacking a tree with a stick. There are three trees in a line along the pavement. Jay swings his stick like a sword, reeling around, running from one tree to another, fighting a battle in his head. It must be good being six—spending half your life in another world where reality can't get you.

Baz asks Mac his next question. *"Fuzzy Logic* was the debut album for which of the following? A: Super Furry Animals? B: Arctic Monkeys? Or C: Frank Zappa?"

"Ah, it's not Frank," says Mac.

"A ZAPPA man, are you?" says Baz. "Don't eat the yellow snow!"

They both laugh. This is it. I'm going out.

"Erm," says Mac. "It's going to have to be a guess. I'll say B: Arctic Monkeys."

The clang of swords again, then a pause. "It's a flesh wound," says Baz. "But you're BOTH STILL BREATHING. *Fuzzy Logic* was in fact the debut LP for Super Furry Animals. Daniel, you're BACK in play!"

I don't believe it! But there's no time to celebrate; Baz is already reading the next question. "Daniel. What element makes up approximately seventy-eight percent of the air we breathe? Is it A: nitrogen? B: oxygen? Or C: argon?"

Oxygen. We breathe oxygen. Surely that's too easy? It must be a trick question. But what if it's not?

I answer before I have time to change my mind. "B: oxygen."

Another clang of metal—it's starting to get on my nerves now.

Baz groans and I know I'm wrong. "You're on SELF-DESTRUCT tonight, Daniel! NITROGEN is the main element, comprising seventy-eight percent of the air we breathe."

I open my mouth to argue, but Baz is already talking to Mac. "It's in YOUR hands now, Mac. This is the closest ANY-BODY has come to defeating our champion. Are YOU—a fellow countryman—the man to do it? What do you think, Mac? DO you feel LUCKY?"

Big surprise, Mac feels lucky. Why wouldn't he? Like Baz said, I'm on self-destruct tonight.

"Here we go," says Baz. "Who wrote the original book from which the film *Coraline* was made? Was it A: Roald Dahl? B: Tim Burton? Or C: Neil Gaiman?"

"I saw that," says Mac. "Good film!"

That's it then. All over.

"You want to know who wrote it? Erm…I'm not sure…
maybe Roald Dahl? No…hang on, I've got a feeling it was
Tim Burton."

"So you're going for B: Tim Burton as the man who
wrote the original story, *Coraline*?"

"Aye."

"Are you sure?"

He's got it right. Baz only asks if you're sure, when you're
right.

"No," says Mac. "But I'll stick with it."

I hear Baz draw breath. Here it comes…

"Mac, I have to tell you that NEIL GAIMAN wrote the
book that inspired the film *Coraline*."

A groan from Mac.

"Come ON, fellas!" says Baz. "This is hardly a good
advert for Scottish brainpower! You know we'll keep going till
somebody gets one right. Even if it does take ALL NIGHT!"

Mac laughs. I don't say anything. My whole body is quivering. I don't know how much more of this I can take.

"Daniel?" says Baz. "Are you still there, my friend?"

"Yeah."

"Come ON, Danny Boy! You're our REIGNING
CHAMPION. You've toyed with the opposition for long
enough—can we FINISH this now?"

"I'll do my best."

"Good man!"

Jay's still fighting the trees. He keeps running back to the
phone box, then darting out to attack, then back, then out
to a different tree. There doesn't seem to be any sequence to

it—sometimes he goes for the same tree, two or three times. I wonder how long it will be before someone comes along and tells him to stop it?

"Daniel. WHICH of the following countries does NOT border France? Is it A: Monaco? B: Andorra? Or C: the Netherlands?"

Geography! Why did it have to be geography?

My mind is blank. No gut feeling, no instinct. Nothing.

I watch Jay fighting the trees. He runs back to the box, then turns to face them again. Three trees. A, B, or C.

"Daniel?" says Baz.

"Yeah."

Jay is poised, stick in hand like a sword, like a mighty claymore. Tree A, Tree B, or Tree C. There can be only one.

"I need an answer, champ."

Jay leaps forward towards Tree B, then swerves round and past it, delivering a slicing blow to Tree C instead.

"Tree C," I tell Baz. "I mean—C."

Baz laughs. "Are you CRACKING under the pressure, champ? WORRIED you might lose your head?"

I manage a strangled laugh.

"Let's get this right. You're telling ME that C: the Netherlands does NOT border the lovely nation of France? Is that correct?"

Jay is smashing the life out of Tree C.

"Yeah."

Silence.

"There can be only one," says Baz, barely above a whisper. "Daniel … you're absolutely RIGHT." The *Highlander* music blasts down the phone. "Mac, my friend—well played. You pushed him all the way—but as we knew at the start, there could BE only one!"

I let Jay stay up late, so he doesn't argue too much when I say it's time for bed. If I'm honest, I want the company. Tonight the flat is too big and too quiet.

I stand at the window and look out over the gray sprawl of Hardacre slowly disappearing in the dusk. Mum's out there somewhere. I know she is. But where? And when is she coming home?

Something flickers in the depths of my brain, a glowing ember of doubt... what if she doesn't?

I shake my head and the glow fades.

You make your own luck—that's what Nanna used to say. She believed that if you expected the worst, that's what you'd get. But if you counted on good things happening, then they usually would. The Power of Positive Thought, she called it.

I wish Nanna was here now. She'd know what to do.

But no amount of Positive Thought is going to make that happen.

THATAWAY

Jay's in a bad mood. He wants to know where Mum is.

It's a good question.

I wish I knew the answer.

I tell him she's working—she had to leave early before he was awake. I even make up a story about her coming in to see him before she went, how we both laughed because he was snoring.

Jay doesn't believe me.

He doesn't say anything though—just scowls and turns up the TV. But the question won't go away.

I've been pretending that everything is normal, for Jay and Nelly and anybody else who might be watching. At least, that's who I thought I was doing it for. Maybe it was as much for me as anyone? Because once you stop pretending, the only thing left is reality—and that's scary.

I go into the kitchen and fill up the kettle. I don't want a drink. I'm delaying, distracting myself from what I should be doing. So I'm almost relieved when the doorbell goes, until my brain throws up a couple of possibilities of who it could be:

The police.

Social services.

It's OK. I don't have to answer it.

The buzzer goes again.

Whoever is out there really wants to come in.

But there's nobody I want to see—except Mum, and she's got a key ... unless she lost it?

Then I hear small feet running up the hall ...

I sprint after him, but it's too late—he's already opening the door.

"Mum!" says Jay.

It takes an age for my eyes to focus on the woman standing in the doorway, then a few seconds longer for my brain to register that the face I'm looking at does not belong to my mother.

"I thought you were my mum," says Jay, shoulders sagging.

Nelly smiles. "Oh, sorry to disappoint you, dear. Is she not at home then?"

"Dunno where she is," says Jay, already on his way back to the television.

"She's at work, I told you," I remind him, for Nelly's benefit.

"On a Saturday?" Nelly's eyebrows attempt simultaneous vertical take-off, so I guess she doesn't believe me.

"Was there something you wanted?" I ask her.

The treacle smile evaporates. "I wish to speak with your mother. What time are you expecting her?"

I shrug, on purpose. "Dunno. She might have to do over-time. Then we're going out, to a friend's house, so we won't be back until late."

"I see."

And I believe she does see—right through me. Nelly doesn't believe a word of it. I wonder if she knows it was me dressed up as Mum who left the Heights yesterday morning.

"Not to worry," she says. "I'm sure our paths will cross before too long." Nelly shows me her teeth. I think it's meant to be a smile, but it doesn't quite make it.

I watch her shuffle towards the stairs.

One push and she'd be down the lot...

Nelly knows Mum's not been here; I'm sure of it. All it takes is one phone call from her and the do-gooders from social services will be round here like a SWAT team.

One quick push and the problem is eliminated.

I could say she tripped. It would be easy.

Do it! Do it now, before it's too late. Do it for Jay.

"Yes?" Nosy Nelly turns, one foot on the stairs.

I realize I've crossed the hall; I'm just an arm's length away. I don't remember leaving the flat.

Nelly blinks, sending tiny crumbs of orange makeup roll-ing down her cheek. There's anger in her eyes, but fear too—as though she could see what I was thinking, what I was going to do.

I shake my head and run back into the flat, slamming the door behind me.

My hands are shaking.

I feel sick.

Was I really going to push Nelly down the stairs? I could have killed her!

But that was the point, wasn't it?

I go to the bathroom and fill the sink, dunking my face in the cold water. I hold my breath until my lungs burn, then lift my head to look in the mirror. The glass is gone, smashed by Mum one drunken night. I'd forgotten, but I'm glad I can't see my reflection—I'm afraid it might scare me.

I try to watch TV with Jay, but I can't concentrate. I keep seeing Nelly at the bottom of the stairs, a red stain spreading out from her head. If she hadn't turned round, would I have done it? Would I have pushed her?

That's another question I can't answer. My head is full of them, hissing and scratching around my brain like the roaches in the kitchen. I want to rip my head off so I don't have to listen to them anymore.

But I can't go on pretending this is normal. Mum's never left us on our own for this long before.

I kept telling myself that she was just out on one of her drinking sessions, that she'd come home after a few days when the money ran out. But she didn't. And now Nelly wants to talk to her and won't stop hounding us until she gets what she wants. I need to find Mum. But where do I start?

What do I know?

Not much. Mum just didn't come home after work on Wednesday night.

But that's a start—the one thing I know for sure.

OK... so why not?

Either something happened so she couldn't come home, or she chose to go somewhere else instead. If Mum had killed herself, or been in an accident, or got arrested, by now somebody would know. The police would have discovered who she was and come round here for me and Jay. Which means Mum didn't come home because she didn't want to.

But where *did* she go?

I start in her bedroom, emptying out drawers, looking under the bed and on top of the wardrobe. I don't know what I'm looking for—anything, I suppose—a clue as to where she might have gone.

The place is a mess of dirty clothes, bottles, and over-flowing ashtrays. It stinks in here too, of stale cigarettes, chip fat, and perfume. Going through Mum's things feels wrong, and I get that crawling feeling up my back that when I turn round she's going to be there in the doorway. Though if she was, I'd be glad—even if she did give me a slap for going through her stuff.

But there's nothing here. Just Mum's rubbish. A pair of muddy shoes in a Parade Wines carrier bag in the corner, a few magazines and old newspapers by the bed, but nothing circled in red pen or intriguingly snipped out. No mysteri-ous letters or receipts, no membership cards for seedy clubs in town. No clues—just stuff. The same as you'd find in any-body's room.

Mum's cleaning overall is on the bed where I left it, but

I can't find her chip shop one. So I know she went to work on Wednesday afternoon. But what stopped her from coming home?

I don't think she planned to go away, because as far as I can see, she didn't take anything with her. If she meant to leave, or if she was planning to ... do something ... she wouldn't have gone to work first. So something must have happened while she was at work—if she even got there. And if she did, what time did she leave? Was she with anybody? I need to find out.

I go back into the front room where Jay is lying upside down on the settee watching *Scooby-Doo*. It's the part at the end of the show when Velma explains how she solved the mystery. *It was easy*, she says. *I just retraced his footsteps, then followed the clues!*

"Are we going to see Mum?" says Jay when he sees the chip shop ahead.

"No, she's at her other job."

"Oh." He looks disappointed.

"Come on, Scoob, remember we've got to look for clues," I say in my best Shaggy-from-*Scooby-Doo* voice.

Of course, now that I actually *want* Jay to pretend he's a dog, he won't have anything to do with the idea. He stares at me like I'm deranged. Maybe I am, for thinking this could possibly work, but I don't know what else to do and I've got to do something.

"You stay here and keep a look-out, Scoob, while I go inside and look for clues," I tell him when we get to the chip shop.

Jay frowns. "I want to come with you. Scooby and Shaggy always stay together."

"They don't allow dogs in there, Scooby old pal!" I'm trying to keep it going, doing the voice and everything; people walking past are staring. "I'll bring you a bag of Scooby Snacks!"

Jay's lip quivers, but eventually he nods. "OK, but don't be too long."

My brother has more in common with that dog than he knows.

The moment I step into Choi's Fish & Chip Shop, my skin tingles and I can feel Mum's presence, though I know she's not here.

Mrs. Choi is shovelling chips into a plastic tray for a bloke in a vest and football shorts. She knows me from the times I've been in to see Mum.

"What happen your mum?" she says, and my heart thuds.

"What do you mean?"

"She no come to work—two days! Salt, vinegar?" she asks the bloke.

I realize Mrs. Choi doesn't know anything. Just that Mum didn't turn up for work. "She's ill," I say.

The bloke turns and looks at me. His face is red, sunburned.

"When she come back to work?"

"I dunno. Soon."

"She no come back soon, I give job to someone else."

Red Face takes his chips and leaves.

"What you want?" Mrs. Choi waits, her scoop poised.

I want to ask questions, but now I'm here I don't know where to start.

"You want something to eat?"

I wonder if she means for free?

"A portion of chips, please."

Mrs. Choi grunts and starts scooping chips into a tray.

"Mum came in on Wednesday, didn't she?"

"Wednesday yes, Thursday no. Salt, vinegar?"

"Please."

She hands me the chips. "One pounds fifty!"

I hear the door open and think it might be Jay, but he's still outside, frowning at me through the window. A woman in sunglasses comes in and stands behind me.

I turn back to Mrs. Choi. "Was she OK? I mean...what time did she leave...on Wednesday?"

Mrs. Choi looks at me. "Same time always."

"Was she with anyone?"

She frowns. "Why you want to know? What happen? Your mum OK?"

"Yeah! She's fine. I mean, she's ill...but..."

Mrs. Choi shakes her head. "She come back Tuesday,

yes? Or I get new girl." She turns to the woman in the sunglasses. "Yes, please?"

I am completely useless. I should have thought about what to ask before we came. It was a waste of time, except for the chips, and I had to pay for those.

We find a strip of shade by the wall of the launderette and sit down. The smell of soap and warm washing mingles with the acid tang of vinegar, but the chips taste good. We're being watched by a ratty brown dog, a string of clear saliva drooling from its mouth.

"Disgusting!" says Jay with admiration, throwing it a chip. The dog hoovers up the food in a single gulp and shuffles a bit closer. I tell Jay to ignore him, so of course he throws it another.

I look around the Parade. Mrs. Choi told me that Mum left work as normal on Wednesday night, which means she was only minutes away from coming home. So why didn't she? Where did she go when she left the chip shop?

If she turned left instead of right, she would have walked by where we're sitting now, then past the post office and the nail bar and on towards the launderette.

"Stupid dog!" says Jay.

The brown dog is chasing a red carrier bag across the pavement, but each time he gets near it, the wind whips the bag away. Jay thinks it's hilarious. Eventually the dog gives up and the bag drifts back down the Parade towards us. It's from the off-licence. There was one just like it in Mum's room...

Parade Wines is empty, except for a scruffy bloke with a silver-gray ponytail buying six cans of lager and a bottle of red wine. I wait for him to leave, then go up to the counter. The man at the till frowns.

"I'll need to see ID if you want to get served."

"I don't want to buy anything, I'm looking for my mum."

He gestures at the empty shop. "She's not in here."

"Not today. Last Wednesday."

"Wednesday?" The man shakes his head. "I wasn't here on Wednesday. That would have been Ann."

"Do you know when she's in next?"

"Who, Ann?"

"Yeah."

"I'll have to check the schedule."

"Thanks." I smile.

He sighs and waddles across to a dog-eared sheet of paper stuck to the back wall. "Ann," he says, running his finger across the sheet. "Monday, Wednesday, Friday. After six."

"Thanks. I'll try then."

He nods, then looks at me suddenly, like he's just noticed I'm here. "Hey, hang on a minute. Why d'you want to know about last Wednesday? That was three days ago. Have you not seen her since then?"

I realize my mistake.

"No! It's not that!" I start to back out of the shop. "It doesn't matter. Thanks for your help."

"Here, watch out!"

The bottles split like bowling pins as I crash into the display. I manage to grab two, but a third squirms out of reach and hits the ground with a thunk! For a second I think it's not going to break; then the glass shatters, spraying wine across the floor in a foaming red river.

I run—dropping the two bottles into a basket on the way out.

"Oi!" shouts the man. "You'll have to pay for that!"

"I haven't got any ID!" I scoop up Jay from the doorway and sprint down the Parade.

I don't stop running until we get to the park.

"Why did you run?" says Jay when I put him down.

"I broke a bottle, by accident."

"Won't you get into trouble?"

I shrug. "Nah!" Though I don't suppose I'll be welcome back there in a hurry. It would have been useful to talk to Ann, but I'm starting to see that asking questions leads to other questions, with answers I don't want to give.

The park is unusually busy. There's a line of trucks at the far end, next to a strange construction of metal tubes and girders. Further along the field, groups of workmen are unloading sections of gray fencing from the back of a truck. They must be getting ready for the festival here tomorrow. I was going to ask Mum if she wanted to go and see the Queen tribute band, but that was before she disappeared.

Jay runs off to go on the slide, then announces the metal is too hot. I remember the man in the chippy and feel the skin on the back of my neck smarting. I should have made Jay wear his cap, or put some sun cream on him...

A picture of Mum suddenly flashes into my head. She's wearing a big straw hat, her face close to mine, laughing as she covers me in sun cream. I can smell it and feel the grittiness of the sand as she rubs it in. That was our last holiday before Jay was born... just me, Mum, and Nanna.

We stayed in this tiny bed-and-breakfast just across the road from the sea and spent every day on the beach. In the evening we'd walk to the funfair at the end of the prom-enade and load up the penny falls. That was when Nanna took me on the dodgems. Mum was too scared, but I loved it—the noise, the smell, the blue sparks dancing over our heads and Nanna crashing into people, laughing like a lunatic. After-wards, we had fish and chips and walked back along the beach while the sun dropped sizzling into the sea.

It seems so long ago, I'm not even sure it really hap-pened. That world doesn't exist anymore. A world before Jay, with Nanna in it, and Mum when she was still happy. Nanna's dead now, and so is the mother I had then. And that kid, the one on the dodgems—where is he?

Jay wants me to push him on the swing. I tell him five min-utes, then we have to go. I want to get back inside. It feels like everyone is watching us out here.

"Are we going to the phone box tonight?" Jay asks as we pass the newsagent's.

"Not tonight." I almost tell him that Baz only does his show during the week, then remember that Jay still thinks I'm phoning a friend from school. I wish I could tell him the truth. A secret is like a bag you have to lug around all the time—each day you add another lie, and it just gets heavier and harder to carry on your own.

"When will Mum be home?" says Jay, as we climb the steps up to the Heights.

"I don't know. Soon."

"I wish she was here now." His hand snakes into mine, all greasy and hot.

"Yeah, me too."

It strikes me that real life isn't like *Scooby-Doo*. There are no conveniently placed clues, no trails of glow-in-the-dark footprints to follow. I think even Velma would struggle to solve this one.

SOMEDAY

"Where's Mum?" Jay looks at me like it's my fault she's not here.

"I told you, she's at work."

Jay shakes his head. "It's Sunday. You don't go to work on Sunday. Angie told me."

Why would Angie tell him that? What's Jay been saying to her?

"Some people work on a Sunday. What about all the people who work in shops?"

"Mum doesn't work in a shop."

"She's got another job, a different one."

"In a shop? Can we go and see her?"

"It's not a shop … and it's not round here. She has to go to another town. She might have to stay there … so it'll just be me and you, on our own for a while." My heart bangs out a warning, but I've got to tell him something.

"She's not going to come home?" Jay's voice quivers.

"Yeah, 'course she will, just not for a few days." I force a grin. "And when she does, she'll have loads of money, so we might be able to go on holiday!" What am I saying? Still, if I'm digging a hole, it might as well be a big one.

Jay's face brightens. "At the seaside?"

"Yeah! But we can't tell anyone."

"About going on holiday?"

"No, about Mum not being here."

"Why not?"

"Because they might think we can't look after ourselves and then they'll make us go and stay with somebody, or get Nosy Nelly to come and look after us. You wouldn't like that, would you?"

Jay pulls a face and shakes his head.

"So you won't tell anyone? Not even Angie."

Another shake. "Unless she asks," says Jay.

"What?"

"I won't say anything unless she asks me."

"No! Don't say anything even if she does ask you."

"But that's telling lies!"

"No it's not! Well... I mean, it's not like a bad lie. It's just not exactly telling the truth."

Jay looks doubtful.

"Look, you don't want Nosy Nelly looking after us, do you?"

Jay shakes his head.

"Well, if you tell anyone that Mum's not here, that's what's going to happen. There won't be anything I can do about it."

Jay frowns and chews his lip. Eventually he sighs. "OK, I won't tell anyone."

We're running out of food. I check what's left in the fridge and the cupboards and put anything edible on the table. It doesn't take up much room.

I wonder how long we could survive on a diet of toast, jam, and Monster Munch.

The remainder of the cash from Humpty is still on the kitchen table. I sort the coins into stacks and count it—twice—but the total doesn't improve. Five pounds and thirty-eight pence. Barely enough to buy food for a couple of days.

This time, going into Mum's room doesn't feel so much like trespassing.

There has to be something here—some clue as to where she's gone.

My Great Plan is falling apart. If I can't find Mum, what use will it be winning the holiday? We can't keep this up forever; someone is going to find out she's not here, and then what?

If you think like that, what hope have you got? says Nanna's voice in my head.

She's right, of course. I have to believe I can find her, even if I don't know how.

I open the curtains to let some light in and start emptying drawers onto the bed. Soon the duvet is strewn with stuff: old cigarette lighters, makeup, bits of jewelry—nothing of any use. There are bags and boxes in the bottom of the wardrobe, mostly clothes and shoes. Mum's knee-length boots are standing in the corner. She loved...loves these boots. I move them to one side and notice that the left one feels heavy. There's something hidden in there—something valuable, it seems.

I don't know what I'm expecting—a jewel encrusted figurine perhaps? The answer to all our problems? Definitely not half a bottle of SavaShoppa Scotch whisky, part of Mum's secret stash. I sit back on my heels, deflated.

I suppose I could sell it, but who to? The only person I can think of is Mum—and that's not even funny.

I slide the bottle back inside the boot and keep searching.

I go through all the pockets of the jeans and skirts and coats hanging in the wardrobe and find another forty-six pence in the lining of Mum's coat. Our new grand total is five pounds and eighty-four pence! I'm ridiculously delighted.

I scan the room; there has to be more money here somewhere.

Mum's old green suitcase is on top of the wardrobe. I dump it on the bed and spring the latch. There's nothing inside except an old T-shirt wrapped around something hard and square. It's a cardboard box full of photographs. I barely recognize the people in the pictures, but I know who they are—mostly Mum and Nanna and a few of my dad. I don't remember him at all. Nanna told me that he and Mum got married when they were really young, when they found out Mum was pregnant with me. Then Dad had an affair with someone else and Mum left him. Two weeks later he was killed in an accident. Nanna said that was when Mum started drinking.

There's a picture of them together: Mum smiling, her arms draped around his shoulders, and Dad looking straight into the camera. It makes the hairs on the back of my neck quiver—it could be me, except for the clothes. I mean, I knew we looked similar, but this is like looking into a mirror. It must be hard for Mum, if I look so much like him.

I drop the photo back onto the pile and notice something underneath, at the bottom of the box. It's a slim red building society book—the account Nanna opened for me when I was born. I'd forgotten all about it. But when I open the book, it's Jay's name printed at the top of the page, not mine. Of course—Nanna opened an account for Jay too. My eyes race down the rows of dates and figures, listing regular monthly payments, usually ten pounds, but a few larger amounts—fifty on Jay's birthday, twenty at Christmas. The balance total is in a box on the right hand side of the page. I have to read it twice to be sure, because the hand holding the book is shaking.

Four hundred and fifty-three pounds, and seventy-six pence!

We're rich!

"Thank you, Nanna!" I kiss the pages of the book, and that's when I notice the next line. The amount is for fifty pounds, only this time the figure is in the withdrawal column. The entry is dated March of last year—but Nanna was dead by then. Jay must have taken it out... but he can't have.

The truth of what has happened slowly settles.

Like ice.

My fingers are trembling as I turn the page and see more rows of figures, all in the withdrawal column—one hundred—fifty—seventy-five! The account balance drops from five figures to three. My eyes dart to the last entry, the total at the end of the line: one pound and ninety-seven pence.

She cleaned it out.

Over four hundred pounds and Mum took the lot!

I stand up and the box falls to the floor, spraying photos across the carpet.

I can't believe she took Jay's money!

I fling the useless book across the room, then turn and drag the quilt off the bed, spilling her things onto the floor. I'm stamping and kicking, grinding her stuff into the carpet, and I can hear a sound—a low growl, filled with anger and frustration. It's only when I stop to listen that I realize the noise is coming from me.

I drop to my knees in the middle of the mess, head in hands—my throat burning, aching with tears that won't come. It would have been better if I hadn't found the book. I'd forgotten they even existed.

I sit up.

I'd forgotten *they* existed!

There were two books! One for Jay, one for me!

I scrabble through the chaos on the floor until I find the box, ripped and half-hidden under the dressing table. It still contains a few photos, but nothing else. So where's the other book? Maybe Mum put it somewhere. Maybe she's got it with her.

What am I thinking? If she took Jay's money, chances are mine's gone too.

Nanna gave us those books when she knew she was dying. I remember visiting her in hospital. Mum went to the toilet, and that's when Nanna gave me the envelope with my book inside. She told me not to tell Mum—which is why I hid it in my Secret Things Tin, in my bedroom. But that was in our old house—what happened to it when we moved?

I run across the hall to the room I share with Jay and start tearing through the chest of drawers, but I know it's not in here.

Think, Laurence. Where did you put it?

We left in such a rush, in the middle of the night ... I remember Mum shouting at me to pack a bag. Anything I couldn't fit in, I'd have to leave behind. What if I left it there? The thought makes me feel sick.

I search every cupboard and drawer and shelf in the room, though I don't hold out much hope. It's just easier to keep looking than accept the fact it isn't here.

But it isn't.

If it was, I would have found it.

Unless ...

I lie on my belly and crawl under the bed, through the sea of lost socks and Jay's discarded toys. I can see something at the back, by the wall ... but it turns out to be my copy of *Treasure Island,* bent and twisted out of shape. It's not here—I'm wasting my time. I start to shuffle back and my foot knocks against something solid in the far corner. It takes an age to turn round, and I can't stop the hope rising in my chest. It's the right shape, and when I reach out, my fingers feel the hard edges of a metal box. I drag it through the dust and out into the light.

My Secret Things Tin.

I hold it in my hands for a moment, not daring to look inside. There's a pebble in here, from the beach at Barmouth where we went on holiday with Nanna, and a note from Chloe Raven asking me to marry her—we were both eight at the time. I could list the contents of this box by heart, but suddenly none of it means anything... except the book.

If it's still in here.

Please let it still be in here.

The hinges creak as I pop the lid. It emits the smell I remember so well: metallic, with a faint tang of the sea. I'm back in my old room... I can hear Nanna downstairs, talking to Mum...

The book is still here.

Still inside the envelope with my name on the front.

But that doesn't mean Mum hasn't already got to it.

I lift the envelope out and slide the book into my lap.

This time the name inside the cover is mine. Again, the rows of regular payments, page after page of them.

My hands are shaking.

I can barely breathe.

I look across to the next column, the one marked *Withdrawals*... but this account has not been touched since the day Nanna made her last deposit.

I wipe the back of my hand across my eyes and read the total in the last line.

One thousand, four hundred and thirty-five pounds.

We're saved!

Pop in the Park has started; we can hear the throb of music from inside the flat. Jay wants to go to the fair—and I did kind of promise to meet Han. Those girls he knows are coming over.

I should be looking for Mum, but it's too late to start now. One night won't make any difference. We deserve to have some fun.

Han is waiting by the gate smoking a cigarette. He nods towards Jay.

"What d'you bring him for?"

"Mum's at work. I had to."

Han frowns, but then his face lights up. "Hey! Girls love little kids, don't they? Nice one, Roach. Good thinking, man." He puts his arm round my shoulders. "I tell you, we're on here, all sorted!"

"Where are we meeting them?"

"Outside the Ghost Train," says Han. "We get them on there, see, it's dark inside—scary—they'll be all over us!" His eyebrows do their wave thing again.

Which is fine, except Jay's too small to go on the Ghost Train and I can't leave him outside. Why can't I ever do anything on my own? Han doesn't have to bring *his* little brother out with him. But then Han's got a mum and dad and a big sister back at home. It's not Jay's fault.

The park is unrecognizable. The scaffolding we saw going up yesterday is now a fully fledged stage—a black shrouded half-dome, flanked on either side by massive speaker stacks and a lighting rig. There's a band on, but nobody seems particularly interested except the handful of friends leaning against the barrier in front.

We head for the fair, threading our way between the bodies scattered on the grass—people in deck chairs, sitting around picnic rugs, or just lying sprawled out in the sun. Jay runs on ahead, towards the cluster of brightly painted wagons and tents at the far end of the field.

There's a line of vans selling burgers and hot dogs, and I'm tempted to get something now, but the food is expensive and we're bound to want to eat later. I'm starting to realize that five pounds and eighty-four pence won't last long in a place like this.

Jay goes straight to the roundabout. It costs a pound for a go—which seems like a lot just to sit in a wooden aeroplane and go round in a circle a few times—but I give him the money. He chooses a red plane with black crosses on the wings. I can see him making machine-gun noises, pretending to shoot people as he goes round.

Next to me, Han is texting frantically.

"They'll be here in fifteen," he says, lighting another cigarette and grinning at me. "I'm telling you, they're hot, man!" Han licks his finger and makes a sizzling sound.

"Why's he doing that?" says Jay, appearing beside us.

"You finished already?"

He nods and points. "I want to go on the roller-coaster."

This one is two pounds. Luckily Jay is too small to be allowed on. I make him stand by the measure on the board to prove it, but he's still not happy, moaning at me like it's my fault.

"I'm hungry," he says, pouting.

We leave Han pacing by the Ghost Train, staring at his mobile. He looks like a train himself, tearing up and down with puffs of smoke rising above his head.

The queue for the chip van is long and submerged in a thick cloud of frying onions. My stomach groans. I read the menu board leaning up against the side of the van and work out the cheapest option. I suggest chips, but Jay wants a hot dog. It'll cost me half of all the money we have, but I want to keep him happy. Once he gets in a bad mood, I might as well give up and go home.

"They're gonna be late," says Han, trying not to look disappointed. "They're gonna meet us down the front."

"OK." I'm glad to get Jay away from the fair before he spots anything else that will cost me money.

We find a space near the front, towards the side of the speaker stack. The band has finished and there are lots of people in black T-shirts moving equipment around on stage.

"This is boring," says Jay. "I want to go back to the fair."

"God, Jay! We've only just got here!"

Jay looks hurt. I feel guilty.

"Sorry ... look, there'll be another band on soon." I smile, but Jay folds his arms and turns his back. I'm starting to think that coming here wasn't such a good idea. The heat is giving me a headache and my stomach feels like it's turned itself inside out, I'm so hungry. Everywhere I look there are people eating: walking past stuffing burgers into their mouths, or sitting on the grass with whole feasts spread out on blankets in front of them.

Han nudges me. "Who's that?"

"What?"

"That girl on stage."

I look up and see a girl in a red and gold blazer waving at me. There's a cluster of people on stage now, all dressed in the same uniform. It's only when one of the men props up a sign saying "Brass-O" that I realize it's the girl from the library. I raise my hand to wave back, but she's already turned away.

"D'you know her then?" asks Han.

"Not really. I only met her once. She goes to our school."

"What's she called?"

"Mina ... something. I dunno."

He shrugs, already turning away, scanning the field for the hundredth time. "Where are they?" he says, mostly to himself.

Brass-O is better than I expect. They play lots of TV themes and famous songs, but all on trumpets and stuff. I watch Mina most of the time, but she doesn't look over again.

They finish with the *Hawaii Five-O* song, and when they leave the stage I feel oddly disappointed.

"That was great!" says Jay, who spent most of the gig perched on my shoulders, hanging on to my hair. Only Han looks miserable.

"No answer," he says, frowning at his phone. "They should have been here ages ago."

"It's getting busy," I tell him. "They could be here already."

"Yeah." Han nods. "I'll text them."

I'm scanning the crowd when I feel a dig in the ribs.

"Don't wave then, will you." Mina is standing next to me, dressed in her Brass-O uniform.

I feel my cheeks flush. "You were great!" I tell her.

She screws up her face. "It was OK, I suppose. I was flat all the way through 'YMCA.'"

"We didn't notice. Jay enjoyed it."

She looks down at Jay and grins. "Little kids and pensioners—they'll clap at anything that makes a noise."

"Mina!" A blonde girl in a vest and tiny skirt pushes past me and hugs Mina.

Han, previously silent and brooding, suddenly looks interested.

Mina untangles herself from the girl and turns to me. "You know Amy, from school?"

The girl looks vaguely familiar.

"This is Laurence Laurence Roach."

Amy nods. "I've seen you around, yeah!"

"I'm Han," says Han, shouldering his way between us.

"Smoke?" He produces his cigarettes with a flourish and promptly drops half of them on the ground.

Amy shakes her head and links arms with Mina. "Come on," she says. "Let's go to the fair."

Han is scrabbling around on the grass trying to retrieve his cigarettes. Jay's helping, while at the same time telling Han that smoking will make him die.

"Come on," says Mina to me. "We're going to the fair. You can buy me some doughnuts, then I might just forgive you for being so rude!"

The fair is a lot more crowded now than it was earlier. Tinny pop songs howl from hidden speakers, fighting the distant thump and crunch of the bands on stage. The air is full of shrieking voices and the scream of the rides. Everything moves. Lights flash and spin, blasting jagged colors through the bodies pushing and pressing in the heat. I hold tight to Jay's hand, following Mina's red jacket through the crush, and wonder what I'm doing here. I feel sick from lack of food and staying too long in the sun. Maybe we should go home. I'm not sure I'm having a good time.

Han seems happy, though. He's magically produced a bottle of vodka from his pocket, which seems to have made him a lot more popular with Amy. The girls are ahead of us, arms entwined, heads together. Han grins and offers me the bottle.

"No thanks."

"Go on, man! It'll help you relax." He nods towards Mina and his eyebrows quiver. "You're in there, man, no sweat!"

I shake my head. "We're just friends."

I'm not even sure we're that. I don't know what we are. I hardly know her.

We're standing outside the Ghost Train. There's an awkward moment when Han and Amy stagger towards the queue, giggling—and Mina stands there looking expectantly at me.

"They won't let Jay on." I shrug. "Sorry."

"Yes they will!" says Jay.

"You're too young."

"No, I'm not!" Jay frowns. "It's not up to you anyway."

I point to the man at the entrance to the Ghost Train. "No, it's up to him."

Jay growls and stamps his foot.

"It's rubbish in there anyway," says Mina, holding out her hand to him. "I know somewhere much better."

Jay takes Mina's hand and sticks his tongue out at me.

She leads us to a grubby-looking tent on the edge of the fair. There's no queue and it's free to go inside. Above the opening is a wooden sign with old-fashioned swirly writing: *Prepare to be amazed! You are about to step into another dimension, a land where the rules of our world mean nothing. You have been warned . . .*

Before I get the chance to ask Mina if she's sure this is a good idea, she grins and disappears inside the tent with Jay.

I hurry after them and nearly collide with a curly haired

midget rushing straight at me. It's only when I jump out of the way that I realize the midget is me. We're in a Hall of Mirrors... well, a Tent of Mirrors, anyway.

Jay and Mina are standing just inside, laughing at me. I can barely see them it's so dark in here. I shiver. Compared to the cauldron outside, the atmosphere in the tent is damp and earthy, with the smell of something slightly sticky in the air.

We follow the faint luminous arrows on the ground into deeper darkness. I can hear Jay and Mina beside me, but only see their reflections—laughing and pointing, coming at me from all sides. One minute I'm small, the next huge, my arms elastic, curving up and over my head. Now Jay towers over me, three times his normal size. Mina is thin, then round and fat like a beach ball. I'm aware of other people in here with us. Shadows and faces flickering in and out of my reflections, upside down, left and right—converging into one person, who smiles and splits in two, each side going in opposite directions. It's making me feel dizzy. I walk over to where Jay and Mina are laughing at a man making faces at Jay. His eyes in the mirror are huge and rolling—he growls like a monster, and Jay screams. The man laughs.

There's something familiar about him, but it's hard to see what he really looks like. I'm sure I've seen him before, though. I probably have—the whole of Hardacre could be here.

The man staggers towards the mirror like a zombie, his gray ponytail shining silver in the lights. This time Jay and Mina both scream, then Jay growls back at the man, finding his giant reflection in the mirror. The man pretends to be afraid, and for a second or two I see the face of a woman, watching.

The blood in my veins turns to ice. I can't move. My eyes are fixed on a dark empty space in the mirror where, a second ago, I'm certain I was looking at a reflection of Mum's face.

I turn round and a trio of midgets stare at me wide-eyed. I lurch, left and right, fighting to see what is real amongst the illusion, but all I find is my own face. I twist in a complete circle, scanning the figures in the tent—flashing faces scream- ing, laughing, vanishing. And for a second I see it again—a glimpse of red hair and eyes looking back at me. A face not smiling or laughing—which is why I notice it—and then it's gone, and I'm not sure it was ever there. Except the cold in my bones, the thundering in my chest, tell me it was. Mum's here. I can feel it.

I race for the exit and stumble, landing on my hands and knees on the damp grass. Then I'm up and through the flap, and the heat and noise of the fair hits me like a wave. Bodies, lights, movement, people everywhere. I push my way through the crowd—first one way, then the other—but I can't see her. Maybe she's still inside. I turn round, and Mina and Jay are standing there frowning at me.

"Laurence! Are you all right?"

I stop. Take a breath and nod. "I'm fine. I just … you know, felt a bit dizzy. All those mirrors."

"You don't look right." Mina steps closer. "You look like you've seen a ghost!" She laughs.

I gaze over the swarming sea of heads and shrug. "Maybe I did."

After the glare of the fairground, the park seems very dark as we weave our way towards the stage. The main band is about to come on—the Queen tribute act. There's a huge painted banner draped behind the drum kit, with *Sheer Heart Attack* written in jagged red capitals. It's the name of a Queen album. I know because they're Mum's favorite band.

I keep telling myself I couldn't have seen her in the Tent of Mirrors. It was just my imagination, the lights and the reflections, the fact that I haven't eaten in hours. I was hallucinating, that's all.

But I'm still searching the shadowy crowd for her, all the way to the front.

I hoist Jay onto my shoulders so he can see better. He's excited at being out so late in the dark, watching the lights pulsing and strobing across the gleaming drum kit; the banks of amps hunkered, humming, ready to leap into life. Han is smoking a cigarette and grinning at me while Amy sits on his shoulders, swigging from the bottle of vodka.

"Glad you came?" says Mina, standing close to me.

I nod. "Yeah. You?"

"I had no choice!" She laughs.

Neither did I, I think as the stage erupts in a blast of white light and the a cappella intro from "Fat Bottomed Girls" erupts from the speakers. The guitar kicks in and the crowd around me goes crazy. Amy whoops and suddenly everybody is moving, bouncing, surging towards the stage. Jay grips my hair in both fists, but I can hear him cheering and whooping, copying Amy.

The band is good—loud and powerful. Pounding drums and a bass that bounces my heart with every beat, while the guitars rip and growl like caged beasts. They sound just like the Queen CD—well, almost. The singer is doing his best, but nobody can sing like Freddie. That's what Mum always says.

I turn to look at the faces around us, illuminated red and green by the stage lights. Then Jay kicks me.

"I can't see!" he says, twisting my head back round by the hair.

I give up. She's not here. Besides, I'm supposed to be enjoying myself.

After five songs I'm drenched in sweat, bruised, and deafened—and loving every minute. On stage the singer steps up to the mic. "How you all doing?" he says, trying to sound like Freddie Mercury but unable to hide his Midlands accent. "Are you having a good time?"

The crowd cheers as the band launch into "Don't Stop Me Now." I've heard the song a million times, but I don't think I've ever really listened before. Maybe it's the darkness, the night air on my face—or maybe it's Mina, leaning against me, her hands holding my arms around her waist. I don't know and I don't care. I feel alive. I'm happy—having a good time, like the song says! And *no*—I don't want it to stop. I *am* floating around in ecstasy—I want to hug everybody. I look at Han and think he's the best friend in the world, Jay the best little brother anybody could wish for ...

And then I see him. I notice because he's moving through the crowd, not looking at the stage. The man from the Tent of Mirrors, the one with the silver hair ... and there's someone with him. I can't see who it is, because of the crowd and the lights, but it's a woman. A tall woman. I lift Jay onto the ground and shout into Mina's ear.

"Can you look after him? I'll be back in a minute."

"Where you going?" shouts Jay. But I'm already pushing through the crush of bodies, my eyes fixed on the silver head moving through the crowd. For once I'm glad to be tall, but I still lose sight of them a couple of times. I'm stumbling, crashing into people, getting sworn at, shoved around, but I don't care—I can't lose them.

It's Mum. I'm sure of it now. Even though I still haven't got a proper look at her. I can feel it—like I did in the Tent of Mirrors, as if there's an invisible rope between us, dragging me after her.

I'm aware the song has finished and the singer is talking again. "This is our last song," he says, and the crowd groans. "So let's make it a good one—I want to see those hands in the air." The drummer starts playing the introduction to "We Will Rock You" and everybody around me starts to clap in time, raising their arms between each beat. Even at six feet tall, I can't see through a sea of waving limbs.

I plough on blindly, in the same direction as before, and suddenly I'm out the other side, in a strange still place to the side of the stage. A giant speaker stack towers into the sky on my left, blocking out most of the stage lights and some of the sound. There's a generator throbbing somewhere nearby and a fleet of trucks waiting beyond the crash barriers, but no sign of the silver-haired man.

I look back down the field at the line of food vans, now closed and dark, and I see him—a flash of silver under the shadow of the hedge.

A moment later everything goes dark. I turn round, and the lights on stage have dimmed to nothing. The crowd is still cheering and clapping, but the field is in complete darkness except for the string of bulbs along the perimeter, barely illuminating the posts holding them up. I wonder what's going on. Then the sky booms and erupts into color, and trails of light fizz across the gasping crowd. I'd forgotten about the fireworks—the big finale.

The sky flashes green and red, and for a moment I see two flickering figures turn and squeeze through the gap between vans up ahead. I shout after them, but my words are lost in the crack of the gunpowder. When I get to the spot there's nothing there. Just a hedge, thick and tall, towering over my head. I wait for the next blast of light just to be sure, but there's nothing, no way out. So where are they? People don't just disappear into thin air.

When the crowd starts drifting past me, I realize the fireworks have finished—the show's over. I have to get back to Jay and Mina.

Once again I find myself walking against a tide of bodies, and I can't see where I'm going. Some people have got torches, but it doesn't help when they shine them in my face and tell me I'm going the wrong way.

Eventually I make it back to the place where I left the others.

Except they're not here. The grass in front of the stage is empty.

I feel sick.

Why did I leave him? What was I thinking?

I start to run—shouting Jay's name. I don't know where I'm going, but I can't stand still.

People are looking at me—laughing and pointing. I stumble through them, all the way down to the fair, then back across the field towards the stage. I trip and fall, my hands slithering through mud and rubbish. I get up and wipe the snot from my face, taste blood in my mouth, and run on. A man in a reflective vest tries to stop me, shining his lantern in my face and telling me I can't go back that way.

"My brother's in there!" I scream, pushing him away and running on.

I skirt the field again, trying to see into the shadows. Then a hand grabs my arm and I twist away, turning, ready to face the man in the vest.

"Laurence!" Mina is standing in front of me. "Didn't you hear me calling?"

"What? Where's Jay?" I grab Mina by the shoulders. "What have you done with him?"

"He's fine. He's with Amy!" She pushes my hands away.

"Where were you?" I shout. "I came back and you'd gone!"

"Laurence," says Mina, putting her hand on my arm. "It's OK. He's fine. Calm down."

I'm shaking.

I take a breath and wipe the back of my arm across my eyes. I realize how I must look, even in the dark—the snot and the tears.

"We had to move 'cause of your mate," says Mina, starting to walk back towards the fairground.

"What d'you mean?"

"Too much excitement, by the looks of him." Mina stops and I see Han beside the Tent of Mirrors, sitting on the grass with his head between his knees.

"You should have seen all the sick!" says Jay, wandering over.

Amy is standing some distance away, not looking too good herself.

"It was right at the end," says Mina, shaking her head. "Last song. I think the hand claps did it for him." She mimes Han clapping his hands above his head, then vomiting onto the ground. "Don't think the bloke in front was too pleased, mind. We had to get him out quick. I'm sorry, I didn't mean to frighten you."

I shake my head. "No! I'm sorry. I shouldn't have left him with you."

"Who, him, or Romeo over there?" She laughs, then frowns. "Where did you get to anyhow?"

I open my mouth to speak, then realize I don't know what to say. How can I explain it? Unless I tell her everything.

A big part of me wants to tell her, but I can't.

So I just shrug and shake my head. It's pathetic. I can't even look her in the eye.

"Right," says Mina. "I should probably get going anyhow. Get her home before she does the same."

I nod. "Yeah! Of course—sorry!"

"Not your fault, Big Man."

"Will you be OK?"

Mina nods. "Dad should be outside. He said he'd pick us up. Just hope Amy doesn't chuck in the car." She nods at Han. "You gonna be all right with Han Solo there?"

"Yeah."

"Right, well—thanks, Laurence Laurence Roach, it's been quite a night, I'll say that for you!" She laughs and puts an arm around Amy, guiding her towards the exit.

I watch them go. I should call after her before it's too late. But what can I say?

"Laurence!" Jay tugs at my arm. "He's being sick again."

Han is doubled over by the tent, coughing and spitting. When I look back towards the gate, Mina and Amy are gone—vanished into the night.

I sigh and walk over to Han.

What is it about me and vomiting drunks? I seem to inspire it in people.

So much for floating in ecstasy. My life's not like that. Never will be.

I should know that by now.

MEANDAY

I could kick myself.

Last night's events keep replaying in my head like a looped video clip. I can hear the canned laughter pasted over the top as I make an idiot of myself over and over again. The picture always freezes on Mina's face, zooming in on that look of exasperation and disappointment she gave me. I don't blame her, though. What was I doing running off like that, with no explanation, to chase two complete strangers around the park?

I was tired? My brain was doing weird things because I hadn't had enough to eat? Or maybe I wanted it to be Mum so much, I believed it was. Taking the Power of Positive Thought a little bit too far.

At least the money is real. I can feel the building society book in my pocket. It helps dull the pain of last night—a little.

This morning we sit on the wall at the end of the Parade and have Monster Munch for breakfast for the last time. I almost feel nostalgic, rinsing the tangy remnants around my mouth with warm lemonade.

After breakfast I walk Jay to school as usual. Just before he goes to line up, I remind him not to say anything to anyone about Mum being away.

"I know. You already told me!"

"Good! Just don't forget."

Jay sighs and rolls his eyes like I'm an idiot.

The bus into town is crowded with people going to work: miserable glazed faces hiding behind newspapers and earphones. I find a seat towards the back and hope nobody I know gets on board. Missing school today will mean Mr. Buchan puts me on report, but it's worth it to get the money. I'll be able to take a taxi to school from now on—that should get me there in time. Who needs superpowers when you've got one thousand, four hundred and thirty-five pounds!

The building society is in the old part of Hardacre. It looks like a mini castle, with tall leaded windows and a dramatic stone arch over the entrance. I heave open the wooden door and stumble inside, my stomach churning like a cauldron.

The place is deserted—cool and silent as a library.

The woman behind the counter looks up and smiles. "Good morning, sir, how can I help?" A silver badge pinned to her lapel says *Sandra*.

"Hello, um … I'd like some money, please." *Smoothly done, Laurence.*

"How much would you like?"

"Er … a hundred, please." That should be enough to pay Angie and leave some for food. But then I'll have to come into town again to get more for next week—and there's the taxis to school … "No, make it two hundred—no, three—please."

Sandra smiles and nods towards the red book I'm clutching. "If I could have your pass book, please, sir."

I slide it through the gap under the glass.

I'll get a taxi back to the Heights and go shopping. Fill up a basket at SavaShoppa, all the things Jay likes. Tonight we'll have the biggest slap-up meal in history! I can't wait to see the look on his face.

"Three hundred pounds, sir?"

"Yes, please."

She opens my book and starts to type something into her computer, then stops. "Ah, how old are you, Mr. Roach?"

I pause for too long to lie. "Fifteen." I know immediately it's the wrong answer.

Sandra closes my book. "Ah," she says, "in that case I'm afraid I can't let you withdraw any money at this time. You need the named person present."

"What?"

"This is a Junior Account—it was opened in your name by an adult. Your mum perhaps?"

"My nan."

Sandra smiles. "Would she be able to come in with you? We need the named person to sign for any withdrawals until you turn sixteen. Then we can transfer your funds into one of our standard saver accounts. You get a cash card with our high interest current account, so you can use any cash machine with a LINK facility."

"My nan's dead."

"Oh, I'm sorry." Sandra looks down at my book. "Was she Mrs. M. Roach?"

"No, that's my mum."

Sandra brightens. "Oh, well, that makes it easier. If your mum is the named person, you just need to bring her down with you and we can get you some money." She smiles and slides my book back across the shiny counter.

I wish I could explain to Sandra how far from easy bringing Mum down here actually is. But I don't. I just take my book, remember to say thank you, and leave.

I thought I would feel angry, but I don't. I'm just tired. I should go to school—tell them I had a dentist appointment or something—but I can't face it right now. So I walk. I don't even know where I'm going, I'm just putting one foot in front of the other.

It's the music that drags me back—the annoying Radio Ham jingle that doesn't quite rhyme: *Number one, for Hardacre and Marston!* I look up and realize I'm standing on the pavement outside the radio station. I must have walked past this place loads of times, but I never really noticed it before. There's not much to see, just a glass front with a huge red and blue logo plastered across it. The sound is coming from tiny speakers above the door, feeding live Radio Ham into the street.

Through the window it looks like a doctor's waiting room, just with better chairs. There's a line of glossy portraits of Radio Ham personalities on the wall. I wonder which one is Baz. I'm too far away to read the labels underneath, even when I press my face right up against the glass and use my hands to block out the sun. The nearest picture is an ancient bloke with gray hair slicked back into an old-fashioned bus driver quiff, but I don't think that's Baz. Next is a woman and a young black guy, then two that could be him. The first looks like a kids' TV presenter, so probably not Baz. Which leaves the fat-faced bloke at the end, with the bad hair and glasses. I'm looking at the face, trying to match it to Baz's voice, when I feel the receptionist scowling at me from behind her desk.

I step back from the glass and carry on walking.

I don't come to the park on purpose. I just end up here.

The hedge doesn't seem as tall or dense as it did last night, and there are gaps where you can see through to the field beyond. I walk along it until I guess I'm roughly at the spot where the silver-haired man and ... whoever was with him ... vanished. There are deep ridges in the grass where the food vans were parked, and a faint aroma of fried onions still hangs in the air. But the thing that clinches it for me is the great big hole in the hedge, like a doorway. I don't know how I missed it—except for the fact that it was so dark last night I could hardly see my hand in front of my face. Also, judging by the position of the tire marks, the gap would have been hidden behind one of the vans. At least now I know I wasn't chasing ghosts.

Branches snatch at my shirt and I have to duck to get through the hedge, but you can tell it's been used before. The grass is trampled down and there are footprints in the mud on the other side. Now I'm through, I can see that it isn't just another field. A few meters in front of me, a line of ducks glide across the oily green surface of the canal. But between where I'm standing and the grassy bank up to the towpath is a ditch full of waist-high grass and stinging nettles. There's a patch without too many stingers, where some of the reeds are bent back as though somebody has recently been through this way.

I take a step towards the canal and my foot sinks ankle-deep into ice cold water. The momentum and the shock propels me forward, and my other foot splashes down before I can stop myself. Now that I'm standing in it, I can see the grass is actually growing out of a shallow stream running along the bottom of the ditch. Both my feet have disappeared beneath the surface. I could go back, but I'm already soaked, and I can't see another way across. I might as well keep going.

I lurch forward, one foot at a time. With each step the mud and weeds suck at my feet and more water seeps into my socks. I peer through the reeds to the dry bank ahead. Not that far now. I lift my foot and my right shoe comes off with a loud shlurp. I waver, balancing on one leg, my shoeless sock hovering above the murky surface. I roll up a sleeve and reach down into the water. It's cold and slimy; I try not to think about what could be in here. Finally my fingers touch something solid and I exhume the shoe—full of gray silty mud and dripping with weeds.

Putting it back on seems the obvious thing to do, until I try it. I feel myself pitch forward and grab at the reeds for support. They sag, then snap and I go down. At least I remember to close my mouth.

I'm sitting up to my waist in freezing cold ditch-water. I can smell it. I can taste the grittiness of it between my teeth and feel it working its way inside my trousers. It's the perfect end to a perfect day, and it's still only lunchtime. I feel the hard edge of the building society book in my pocket and reach down to rescue it, then remember it's useless to me anyway. I think I'll just sit here. I don't care if the water is seeping into my pants. I don't care how cold and slimy it is. This suits me fine.

"Laurence?"

There's a squeal of brakes and I look up, squinting into the sun at the silhouette on the towpath. I can't see who it is, but the voice is unmistakable.

"What you doing?" says Mina, dropping her bike and coming down the bank towards me.

"Nothing."

Mina puts her hands on her hips and looks at me.

"Are you just going to sit there?"

I shrug. "What are you doing here, anyway?"

"It's lunchtime. I was just going home."

That means it's gone one o'clock. I must have been walking round for hours.

"Did you come through the hedge?" says Mina after a moment. "Were you trying to get to the canal?"

I nod, not looking at her.

"Why didn't you use the bridge?"

"What bridge?"

"That one there." Mina points towards a low gray slab of concrete about ten meters to my right. It's partly hidden by the undergrowth, but visible enough now that I know it's there.

She comes to the edge of the bank and sits down. "You're a weird lot down here. I thought people would be the same wherever, but they're not."

I can feel her watching me, but I can't look at her. I wish she'd just go and leave me to rot.

"Anyhow, I wouldn't stay there too long," she says.

"Why not?" I'm still not looking at her.

"Well … ditch worms, for a start."

"What?"

"Ditch worms. You get them everywhere."

"What are ditch worms?" I ask, feeling the mud oozing between my legs.

"About so long." Mina holds her thumb and forefinger about eight centimeters apart. "They live in the mud, at the bottom of ditches—hence the name. Most of the time they stay there, minding their own business like, feeding on dead fish carcasses and stuff—they're carnivores, see. The only time they come out is if someone disturbs the burrow. That's why fishermen wear waders—you know, those big gum boots that go right up your thigh. My uncle said a mate of his got a ditch worm down his boot one time. All he felt was a little nip, like he'd trod on a stone or something, but the worm lays its eggs, see. The bloke's foot swelled up like a golf ball! My uncle said you could see all these little worms squirming about under the surface of the skin. His mate had to go into hospital to get them cut out. The doctor said he was dead lucky the worm hadn't gone up his bum ... "

I stand up in one almighty wave of mud and water and make the bank in two strides. Mina shrieks and dives out of the way. I can feel ditch worms inside my trousers, crawling across my thighs, a whole nest of them squirming between my toes.

I'm hopping around the bank, pulling off my socks, scrubbing my feet on the grass. I'd take off my trousers if Mina wasn't there, watching me and laughing.

Then I stop ... as it hits me. "You made that up, didn't you?"

She can barely speak for laughing. "Got you out though, didn't I."

I sit down on the grass and throw a muddy sock at her. Then I start to laugh—I can't help it. I realize I must have looked pretty funny.

Mina shakes her head. "You're a strange one, Laurence Laurence Roach. Mad as a box of frogs."

And suddenly I don't feel like laughing anymore.

I stare at the ground between my filthy feet and tear out a handful of grass. "Sorry."

"What for? I didn't say it was bad, did I? I like mad people. It's the sane ones I don't trust."

When I look up, Mina is smiling; it's like the sun coming out from behind a cloud.

I need to take my clothes to the launderette, but of course we haven't got any money. So I fill the bath with hot water and shampoo and dump them in there. All the time I'm thinking about Mum and the silver-haired man, wondering if the woman I saw in the park was really her. Because when I went through the hedge by the canal, I got that feeling—like I did walking into the chip shop—that Mum had been there before me. It sounds crazy, I know—but what else have I got? I have to believe that Mum is out there. If it *was* her with the silver-haired man, then she's close. I could find her.

I'm desperate to go back to the canal and start looking, but there isn't time now. I need to get Jay from the House of Fun, and then work out what the hell we're going to eat tonight.

Baz is talking, but I'm not really listening. My eyes are fixed on the windows of our flat. Jay is up there on his own watching television. He wouldn't come down to the phone box with me tonight. I won't be gone long, but it doesn't feel right, especially after what happened last night, and I can't concentrate.

Baz asks me if I feel lucky.

I manage not to laugh.

"OK, then, Daniel—FIRST question. The spectacular natural phenomenon known as the Northern Lights also goes by another name. Is it A: Aurora Borealis? B: The Golden Compass? Or C: El Niño? I'll read those again for you…"

I know it's not B—at least, I don't think it is. But the other two…I think I've heard of El Niño, but I'm not sure. I'll go with that. *Trust your gut, Laurence.*

"What do you reckon, champ?" Baz is waiting for an answer.

"A! The first one!" *Trust my gut today? Not likely.* Given the decisions I've made in the last twenty-four hours, going the exact opposite to my gut seems the safest option.

"Daniel," says Baz after a pause. "So, you're telling me that A: Aurora Borealis, is ANOTHER name for the Northern Lights? Is that right?"

"Yeah." It feels like the drummer from *Sheer Heart Attack* is trapped inside my chest.

"You're quite right, my friend. Aurora Borealis IS another name for the Northern Lights. Did you KNOW there is in fact a southern equivalent? It's called the Aurora AUSTRALIS…" Baz lurches into an appalling Australian accent. "Will you look at the lights, Sheila, strewth!" Then back in his normal voice. "Both phenomena result from ATOMS colliding in the upper atmosphere, becoming ENERGIZED and giving off ENERGY as light. SEE! This isn't just a GREAT show PACKED with some FANTASTIC music, witty banter, and AMAZING competitions—it's EDUCATIONAL as well!" Baz triggers his *Crowd Go Wild* sound effect.

"Question number TWO!" he says. "Continuing on a

CULTURAL theme... you're obviously an educated fellow, Daniel... have you got any letters after your name? Are you a UNIVERSITY man?"

University? I haven't done my GCSEs yet. "Er ... no—"

"Ah, a graduate from the SCHOOL OF LIFE, just like yours truly!"

"Yeah." I'm picturing Baz in the studio: the round face and glasses, the long straggly hair.

"Good man!" he says. "Only you might wish you HAD done a degree in English when you hear the next question." Cue *Collective Gasp from the Crowd.* "Daniel, who WROTE the following famous words..." Baz clears his throat. "*No man is an island, entire of itself; every man is a piece of the continent, a part of the main.* " He pauses. "Hey! That was pretty GOOD! Cheryl—come on, admit it. You were touched by that."

"Not bad," says Cheryl.

"NOT BAD! My, you're a hard woman to please!" Baz laughs. "So, Daniel, my question to YOU is—which GENIUS OF THE QUILL scribed those words so that I could speak them TONIGHT, here on the wireless for YOUR listening pleasure? Was it, A: T. S. Eliot? B: John Donne? Or C: William Shakespeare?"

I haven't a clue. Mr. Buchan would know. It's a pity I don't have his brain to go with the voice.

It could be Shakespeare... it *sounds* like Shakespeare, but maybe that's too obvious—like the oxygen question. I'm not falling for that again. A, then. But the last one was A—they never have two the same, one after another. Which leaves B: John Donne.

Baz is waiting for an answer.

"B!" I blurt out, before I can change my mind.

"CORRECT!" says Baz. "Seventeeth-century metaphysical poet Mr. John Donne is INDEED responsible for those wonderful words of wisdom."

I lean my forehead against the cool glass of the phone box and force myself to take a breath. I need to calm down. I'm nearly there. Somehow, by some incredible dose of good fortune, I've guessed right—twice.

"OK!" says Baz. "Enough culture for one night I think. My BRAIN is beginning to hurt. Let's have a nice sport question."

Of course.

What else would it be?

"Great!" I hear myself saying into the telephone.

"Right then, HERE we go—question number three, and remember … get THIS one right and you're THROUGH, with only THREE more days to go! I BET you can already feel the sand between your toes, can't you, Dan?"

"Not quite." *The only thing I can feel between my toes right now is mud from the ditch by the canal …*

"Soon, my friend, very SOON! SO … are you ready?"

"Ready," I lie.

"Ah, you'll LIKE this one," says Baz. "And you have to BELIEVE me when I tell you—I don't choose these questions. I JUST read them out! If you want to BLAME anybody, blame Cheryl!" He laughs. "Seriously though, Daniel, as an ENGLISHMAN to a Scotsman, I'm NOT asking you this question to rub salt into bitter wounds, HONESTLY! It's what's on the screen, OK?"

"OK." *Just read the question—please!*

"OK, here goes … Which Football League club did goalkeeper Gordon Banks play for when he WON the World Cup with ENGLAND in 1966? Was it A: West Ham United? B: Manchester United? Or C: Leicester City?"

Baz is still apologizing, going on about Scotland and football—stuff I couldn't care less about. Meanwhile my heart is doing cartwheels because I know the answer. I don't have to guess. I don't even have to *ignore* my guess. I know it!

"C, Baz," I say, interrupting him in mid-flow. "Gordon Banks played for Leicester City."

Silence from Baz. A long silence. Dead air. But I know I'm right.

Han is a massive Leicester City fan—he's supported them all his life. He's always going on about it. Sometime or other, Han told me about Gordon Banks. I don't remember when, or why I remembered the fact. But who cares! It went in and stayed.

"BACK of the net!" says Baz, accompanied by the roar of a crowd. "You're going to get some STICK from your fellow countrymen for knowing that!"

"I've got a mate who's a big Leicester City fan."

"Ah! That explains it. What's his name? I imagine you'll be buying him a drink next time you see him!"

I think of Han on his hands and knees by the Tent of

Mirrors, spitting regurgitated vodka into the grass. "Yeah, he likes a drink."

"What's his name? Will he be listening?"

His name? My heart thuds. "Freddie," I say. "Er...I don't know if he's listening."

I hope not.

I search the flat and find seventy-three pence between the sofa cushions in the front room and some copper under Jay's bed. I add what's left from last night, and there's just enough for one SavaShoppa bargain pizza. When I unwrap it, the cardboard base is thicker than the pizza and probably more nutritious.

I put the pizza in the oven and drop the base on top of the tower of rubbish growing out of the bin. Straight away the stack starts to shift, and before I can do anything, the whole lot slides onto the floor. There's stuff everywhere: baked bean cans leaking thick red gloop, the black skin of a banana I remember eating a week ago, wine bottles, bits of crumpled-up paper—it's a mess.

I swear and start to pick up the rubbish, ramming as much as I can back into the bin. There's a soggy cigarette packet and a scrunched-up piece of paper by the sink. I notice the edges of the paper are black and crumbly, like someone tried to set fire to it. Which seems a strange thing to do, so I open up the sheet and smooth it out. It's a letter addressed to Mum—typed and official-looking.

Dear Mrs. Roach, Thank you for attending the interview

for the position of Mr. Parker's Personal Assistant. I'm sorry to inform you that on this occasion you were unsuccessful. It was a very strong field and a hard choice. We did feel, however, that your past experience … there's a hole in the page where the next word should be. A perfect circle the exact diameter of a cigarette, surrounded by a halo of brown scorched paper. There are a dozen of them, peppering the sheet like bullet holes, with a concentration of fire where the author of the letter signed her name.

Now I remember: Mum had a job interview a few weeks ago at an office in town. She came home dead excited, said the interview had gone really well. The job was hers—that's what the woman had said. I look at the ugly rash of cigarette burns obliterating the signature. The job paid double the money Mum was getting from the chip shop and the cleaning job combined. She said we'd be able to look for somewhere better to live, maybe even go on holiday.

But she didn't get it.

I'm sorry to inform you …

Why didn't she tell me?

Then a thought grabs my heart, holding it still for a beat while my eyes travel up to the date on the letter. Last Monday. Which means it would have been here, waiting for Mum when she got back from her cleaning shift on Wednesday morning. The day she disappeared.

I sit down at the kitchen table and stare at the scorched sheet in my hand. It's like one of those pictures you have to look at for ages before you can tell what it is. At first, all you see is loads of dots and squiggles, patterns of color. Then all of a sudden—snap—there's a picture. And it's so obvious you don't know how you ever missed it.

Now I can see everything…

Mum gets home after her shift last Wednesday. She's hungover, tired, hungry. She picks up the post on her way in, sees the letter, and her mood changes in an instant. This is it. The job she's been waiting for. The job she was promised. She's cleaned her last toilet!

Mum tears open the envelope, standing here in the kitchen, right where I am now.

She reads it through twice, just to be sure. There has to be some mistake.

But she knows there isn't.

She throws the letter onto the table and lights up a cigarette… pours herself a drink, then picks it up again. She reads it through—swears—then holds the tip of her ciggie to the paper, right where that cow who promised her the job has signed her name. She watches the paper discolor, a wisp of smoke rise, and then a hole appear—a perfect circle ringed with black. She keeps doing it, swearing as each hole burns through, until she gets bored, crumples the letter up, and dumps it in the bin.

So now I know.

That job was her way out—an escape from a life she hated.

But when she didn't get it, she went anyway.

Because she couldn't take anymore.

So now I know.

"Why are you crying?"

I look up and Jay is in the doorway. I wipe the back of my arm across my eyes. "I'm not. It's hay fever."

Jay looks at me and wrinkles his nose. "What's that smell?"

The pizza!

I grab a tea towel and yank open the oven door. The pizza is a smoldering wreck, burnt beyond recognition, completely uneatable. Of all the things that have gone wrong today, this is the one that breaks me. I sink to my knees on the kitchen floor, the smoking pizza still in my hands, tears streaming down my face. After a moment I feel Jay's arms round my neck, and his voice, small and scared, in my ear.

"Don't cry, Laurence. It's only pizza."

If only that were true.

DUESDAY

"Eat your breakfast, Jay."

A crust of toast smeared with strawberry jam—it's all we have.

"My tummy hurts!" Jay looks at me through creased eyes, clutching his belly.

"Do you need a poo?"

He shakes his head and sniffs. It's the noise he makes when he's getting himself charged up ready to cry. I look across at him and his face is such a cartoon of misery, I laugh.

Jay scowls. "It's not funny!"

"I know—I'm not laughing at you." But I can't help it. I mean, he couldn't look any more fed up if he tried.

And then he bursts into tears.

I kneel down and try to cuddle him, but he punches me.

"Go away, I hate you!"

"Jay, I'm sorry, I wasn't laughing at you," I say, trying to keep my face straight.

I put my arms round him and after a few minutes he stops struggling. He feels hot and sweaty and his hair smells like wet dog.

"I want Mum," he mumbles into my neck. "When's Mum coming home?"

"I don't know."

"I want her to come home now!"

"I know." I hesitate. "She can't … at the moment. She needs to be somewhere else, so she can earn some more money." I'm thinking on my feet—my knees actually—making this up as I go along.

How do I tell him that I don't think she's ever coming home?

I think it will be safer if Jay doesn't go to school. In this sort of mood I don't know what he might say. I can see him now, getting all upset and telling Miss Shaw that he's missing Mum—how he hasn't seen her for days, that it's just me and him on our own at home. How long then before the Do-Good Squad arrive with their clipboards and their insincere smiles?

If Jay doesn't go, it means I can't either. But what does it matter if Mr. Buchan does put me on report? Going to school suddenly seems a lot less important than working out where our next meal is coming from.

The cremated pizza is still lying on the table. Looking at it makes my stomach churn. Two floors directly below me, the shelves of SavaShoppa are stacked with food. Fat bags of crisps and slabs of chocolate; piles of frozen pizza glistening with frost; boxes of crunchy cereal and row upon row of soft white bread. My mouth starts to water.

It's wrong. All that food down there, while up here we're slowly starving to death.

I make a decision.

"Jay, I'm just going down to the shop. I'll be back in a minute. OK? Don't leave the flat."

SavaShoppa is quiet, just me and an old lady with her basket balanced on top of one of those tartan shopping bags on wheels. She looks like she'd fall over if she didn't have the basket to lean on. I can only see two members of the staff—a woman on the till and a bloke in a green SavaShoppa jacket putting milk into one of the fridges; he looks bored, half-asleep.

Now that I'm here, I don't know if I can do this. I've never stolen anything in my life. Apart from that time I took some crayons from nursery school. I felt so guilty then that I burst into tears and confessed everything to Mum.

But this is different.

I'm hungry.

Jay's hungry.

I have to do it.

My hands are sweating. I wipe them on my jeans and walk down the bread and cakes aisle for the third time. The bloke stocking the milk fridge glances up at me, so I turn round and walk back the way I've just come. I couldn't look more suspicious if I was wearing a mask and carrying a bag with SWAG written on it.

I need something small, something I can slip into my

pocket and just walk out of the door with. How hard can it be?

Deep breath.

Come on, Laurence, you can do this.

I pause by the chocolate. It's the right size, but not exactly nutritious. Biscuits? Too big. I should have worn a coat, but how suspicious would that have looked in this heat?

As I walk past the tins of soup, my stomach gurgles lustfully. I lift a can of Chunky Vegetable off the shelf and hear the contents slosh around inside, but it won't fit into my pocket. I move on. Bread? Too bulky. Cereal, milk, pizza—forget it. This is stupid. I go back to the chocolate.

Two king-size Mars bars—one for me, one for Jay. There must be some goodness in them.

I glance over to the checkout. The woman on the till is restocking the cigarettes. The bloke with the milk has gone back into the store room.

I can see the door. Twelve paces and I'll be outside.

I take a step and hear a crash. Something hard lands on my foot.

"Ooh, I'm sorry, dear, are you all right?" Tartan Trolley Lady is looking up at me, the contents of her basket scattered at my feet. "I'm so clumsy these days."

"It's OK!" My heart is banging and my foot throbs where a tin of tuna cat food landed on it.

"I'm ever so sorry." She's trying to bend down to pick up her things, but at the current rate of descent it will be dark before she manages it.

I do it for her—pick up the spilled shopping and put it back in the basket.

"Thank you, dear, thank you, you're very kind." She smiles, then points at the two Mars bars in my hand. "Let me get those for you. It's the least I can do in the circumstances."

"No, you don't have to do that, I'm fine, thanks." Fine? How could I be fine? I'm an idiot. She just offered to buy me food!

Luckily she insists.

Back outside, holding two bars of chocolate in my hand, I look up at the sky and nod a silent thank you. I realize how close I was to making a huge mistake. What if I'd been caught? What would have happened to Jay then?

I bound up the stairs two at a time, my mouth full of creamy chocolate and caramel. My teeth are screaming but I don't care. I'm thinking that maybe my luck is finally changing.

Then I reach the hallway and see that the door to our flat is wide open ...

Jay!

I run in shouting his name. He appears, looking worried.

"What's going on? You left the door ... "

Nosy Nelly emerges from the bathroom and sees me. "Oh, it's you."

"What's going on? What are you doing in my flat?"

Someone else appears behind Nelly: Mr. Dawson from next door. I know who he is because he's been round to complain a few times when Mum was playing music too loud, or last time, when she smashed the bathroom up. He's drying his hands on a towel.

"The plug was in," he says to Nelly, then notices me.

I glance behind him into the bathroom and see that the floor is shiny with water.

"It's dripping through my ceiling," says Nelly. "I'll be sending the repair bill directly to your mother."

"What?" It's taking a while for my brain to put all the pieces together.

"Someone left the tap on the sink running and the plug in," says Mr. Dawson. "It overflowed and started leaking through to downstairs."

"Oh!" I look for Jay, who has suddenly disappeared. "Sorry. Jay must have left the tap running."

"What was he doing here unsupervised?" says Nelly. "That's what I want to know. What if he'd started a fire? What then?"

"How can you start a fire by leaving a tap running?"

"Don't get smart with me, young man!" she says. "You know precisely what I mean. Where's your mother? And why aren't you both at school?"

"At work. School's closed."

"I beg your pardon?"

I sigh elaborately. "Mum is at work and there is a staff training day at school, so we don't have to go in."

"So *you* were supposed to be caring for your little brother then?"

"Yeah."

"Not doing a very good job, were you?"

"I only went down to the shop for some food."

Nelly tuts and turns to Mr. Dawson. "It's not right, leaving a child to look after a child."

Dawson nods. "Some people shouldn't be allowed to have kids."

They're talking like I'm not here, like I'm invisible. Or maybe it's just that I don't count because I'm a kid. What I think or feel doesn't matter.

"Have you seen the state of this place?" continues Nelly. "It's disgusting. I fear for these children's health. I wouldn't be surprised if there's an infestation. Have you seen the kitchen?"

It occurs to me that Nelly has probably had a good snoop around while Dawson fixed the Great Flood. I've had enough.

"Get out!"

Nelly stops mid-sentence and they both stare at me, all wide eyes and open mouths.

"I beg your pardon?"

"Get out of my flat. Now!" I point towards the open door. Dawson looks worried. For once I'm glad to be six foot and slightly scary looking.

Nelly's not so easily put off. She narrows her eyes to bloodshot slits and leans towards me.

"You've not heard the last of this, young man." She prods me in the chest with a bony finger. "Not by a long chalk."

I'm shaking as I stand in the doorway and watch them

leave. I should have pushed the old cow down the stairs when I had the chance.

Jay's hiding under his duvet in our bedroom. He bursts into tears when he sees me.

"I'm—sorry—Laurence," he says, between sobs.

"It doesn't matter." I sit down on the bed.

"When's Mum coming home?" Jay shuffles next to me, a sweaty ball of heat.

"I don't know." I'm too tired to lie anymore.

But I lied to him just then, didn't I? When I told him it didn't matter. It does matter. Nelly was dangerous enough before. Now I get the feeling we're really getting on her nerves.

I must have fallen asleep, because the doorbell wakes me up. I'm on Jay's bed and my arm has gone numb where I've been lying on it. The buzzer goes again, then a knock. Impatient. Insistent. It's probably Nelly coming to complain about something else. Whoever it is, I don't want to speak to them. We're not in.

Then I hear the letterbox go, and a slap as something hits the lino in the hall.

I wait and listen for a while before going to see what it is. The envelope is addressed to Mum, but I open it anyway.

I was right about it being from Nelly.

Words fly off the page like darts ... *children ... unsupervised ... neglect ...* Nelly details the Great Flood and asks Mum to go and see her. Then the part that makes me go cold: *I feel it is my duty to inform the relevant authorities…*

So that's it.

Mum's gone and now Nelly is going to tell social services.

I mash the letter into a ball and throw it down the hall.

"Why do I have to come to the stupid phone box?" says Jay, stamping on every step down from the Heights.

"Because last time I left you on your own, you flooded the flat!"

"Didn't! Anyway—"

"It's not up to me. I know."

Jay growls and stops walking.

"Come on, Jay. Please."

"I'm hungry."

"I know. So am I …" I'm tempted to give in and go back to the flat. What's the point in winning the holiday if Mum's never coming back home?

But I need to get out of there for a while. I can't stand just sitting at home waiting for the knock on the door. I'll probably lose tonight, anyway, so I might as well get it over with.

I crouch down next to Jay. "Just one last time, I promise. Please, Jay."

Jay frowns and chews his lip. "You have to buy me some Pokémon cards."

"OK." I can't afford a packet of Pokémon cards, but what's one more lie?

There's already somebody in the phone box, but it's all right, we've got a few minutes.

Then I see who it is.

Bartman registers us at the same time. For a fraction of a second he looks surprised, maybe even a little scared, and then he smirks. I'm just debating whether to wait or give up and go back to the flat when he finishes his call and puts the receiver back onto the cradle. We wait for him to come out, but he just stands there in the box with his arms folded, staring at us.

I step forward and shout through the glass. "Excuse me, but if you've finished, I need to use the phone."

"Really? That's a shame," he shouts back.

"What's he doing?" says Jay.

"He won't come out."

Jay walks over and tries to open the door, but it's too heavy for him. So he bangs on the glass. For a moment Bartman looks worried; then, when he sees that Jay can't get to him, he starts to laugh.

"We need to use the phone," shouts Jay, pointing.

Bartman shakes his head.

Jay bangs on the glass again, harder this time. "It's important!" he shouts, no doubt seeing the chances of another pack of Pokémon cards slipping away.

Bartman shrugs.

Jay growls and kicks the door ... then bursts into tears.

Bartman thinks this is hilarious, until two blokes walk past and give him a funny look. Jay is now pounding the walls of the phone box, screaming, "Get out! Get out!"

Inside, Bartman is starting to look uncomfortable. Jay's got him cornered, but he's probably too scared to come out now.

I step forward and lift Jay, still kicking and shouting, out of the way.

Bartman looks at me then opens the door, keeping his eyes fixed on Jay. "Sorry. I didn't mean to make him cry."

I don't say anything, just shake my head and step into the phone box. Once the door is closed, I put Jay down. "You OK?"

Jay's red, tear-stained face looks up at me and grins. "Got rid of him, didn't we!"

I laugh as I dial the number for Radio Ham. After all that, I hope we're not too late.

It rings for ages before somebody picks up.

"Hello! It's Daniel Roach, for *Baz's Bedtime Bonanza*."

"Hello?"

"Hello—it's Daniel Roach. I'm a contestant on *Baz's Bedtime Bonanza*. The quiz. Sorry, I'm a bit late."

There's a pause, then a voice I don't recognize. A very old voice, cracked and distant. "Who do you want, dear?"

"It's OK, sorry. Wrong number."

"Is that Bill?"

"No, it's Laur—Daniel…I've got to go, sorry!" I put the phone down and feel terrible.

"Who was that?" says Jay.

I shake my head and start to dial again, then stop—my fingers hovering over the characters etched into the keypad but gone from my brain. I've forgotten the number. I put the receiver back onto the cradle and take a breath. *Calm down. You know it. You dial it every night.* Except I don't—my fingers just know where to go—at least they did until now.

A cold line of sweat trickles down my spine.

Don't think. Just do it.

I pick up the phone and dial.

"Hello? Bill? Is that you?"

I slam the phone down and scream. It rings almost immediately, making me jump.

"Hello?" I say, expecting the old lady to still be on the line.

"Hi, this is Cheryl from Radio Ham. I'm looking for Daniel Roach?"

"Cheryl, hi, it's Daniel," I say, remembering my accent just in time.

"Hi, Dan! Sorry, that didn't sound like you just now!"

"Sorry, um ... I was eating!"

"Oh, OK—are you ready to go on? The quiz is about to start."

"Yeah. I've been trying to ring—I couldn't get through."

"Not to worry. I thought I'd better call you. We couldn't start without our champion."

Ten minutes later I'm walking back along the Parade with Jay, and I can't stop grinning. I'm through to the next round. After the shaky start, everything went really well. Maybe I relaxed because I didn't care. I got one wrong, but the challenger was useless, so I won anyway.

It sounds stupid, but it almost feels like I can't lose. As though I'm meant to win that holiday for Mum. Like a sign—telling me not to give up because there's still hope, there's still me and Jay. Without Jay, I'd have given up tonight. Just walked away.

I put my arm round his shoulders as we climb the steps back up to the Heights. "Thanks for your help tonight. I couldn't have done it without you."

Jay shrugs. "That's OK. You can buy me some Poké-mon cards tomorrow."

"Yeah!" I laugh. "I suppose I'd better."

ENDSDAY

Dear Mrs. Ellison, I'm sorry about the flood. The boys tell me it was an accident and Laurence only went down to the shop to buy some food. I will be happy to talk to you at the weekend, but I'm working lots of overtime this week, so it will be difficult to see you before then. Please don't inform the authorities until we have talked. Yours sincerely, Margaret Roach.

I chew the end of the pen. The letter still doesn't sound right, but it's taken me an hour to get this far. I don't like *Please don't inform the authorities*—it sounds scared, plus I don't like begging Nelly. But maybe that's what I need to do. Make Nelly feel like she's in control, that she has power over us—she'll love that. I add a line in, before the begging bit: *You are right. I should not leave the boys on their own in the flat, but Laurence is normally very good at looking after Jay. I have told him to be more careful.*

I write it all out again and fake Mum's signature at the bottom—I've done it loads of times, on letters to school that Mum was too drunk to sign. I'm still not sure it's going to work, but I don't know what else to do.

We haven't got any envelopes, so I fold the paper in half and write *Mrs. Ellison* on one side, then slip it inside the building society book on Mum's dressing table. Luckily the book dried out OK. Some of the ink has run and the edges of the pages are a bit wrinkly, but it survived. This is good, because I need it for Part One of the Great Plan: Getting Some Money. And if Mum needs to be there to take the money out, then Mum will just have to be there.

The skirt doesn't look too bad, but my hairy legs definitely spoil the effect. I turn away from the mirror and look through Mum's drawers for a pair of tights. I've never worn tights before, and I put a massive tear in the first pair trying to get them on. I'm more careful the second time and manage to get the tights onto my legs without any damage—except now, the crotch part is hanging just above my knees. After a lot of tugging and wriggling I pull them into the right position. It feels weird, but my legs do look a lot better.

Now for a top. Mum doesn't go much for flowery feminine clothes. She dresses like a man most of the time, but that's not going to help *me* look like a woman. The best thing I can find is a white blouse with tiny blue flowers. The buttons do up the wrong way, so it takes me a while to get it on. It doesn't look too bad . . . but there's still something not quite right. But what?

Then I see the lacy black bra on the floor by the bed.

No way!

But if I want this to work . . .

It takes me an age to get the stupid thing on, because it does up at the back. In the end I take it off, fasten it and then pull it on over my head. It has to be the most uncomfortable thing I've ever worn. The lace itches and the straps cut into my shoulders. I don't know how Mum does it. I stuff the bra with the ripped tights and some socks, then check the effect. It looks like I'm trying to smuggle potatoes down my top. I need something less lumpy.

The only thing I can find is a huge jar of lavender bath salts that must have belonged to Nanna. I fill two socks with them, fold over the ends, and slip them into the bra cups. The effect is actually quite realistic, except one is noticeably larger than the other. I even them out and try again. It'll have to do. I smell quite … flowery as well now, which can't be a bad thing.

I take Mum's black Puffa jacket from the cupboard and put that on. It might look a bit odd in this weather, but it puts another layer between the public and my bath-salt boobs. I try to squeeze my feet into Mum's long boots, but they're miles too small. I'll have to make do with shoes. I get the feeling people won't be looking at my feet anyway.

I check the final effect in the mirror. It's definitely better with the sunglasses on. They're huge and hide most of my face. Luckily I don't really have to shave yet, and, with the wig and the sunglasses plus a good smear of Vampire's Kiss, I almost look like a woman. But will *almost* be enough?

It has to be. All we had to eat yesterday was one Mars bar each. It feels like someone is sticking knives into my gut, and it's swollen up like a balloon. At least I'll have Jay with me—that will make it look more believable. Most people give Jay all their attention anyway; they probably won't even notice me.

Jay falls off the settee when I walk into the front room, then bursts out laughing. "You look like Mum!" he says, rolling about on the floor.

That's good. If Jay thinks I look like Mum...this might just work.

"We need to go into town," I tell him.

"Why?"

"To get some money out, so we can buy some food."

"And some Pokémon cards," says Jay. "You promised!"

"Yeah. I know."

"But why are you dressed up like Mum?"

"Because Mum hasn't got time to go to the bank, and they won't give the money to me. Mum said I could pretend to be her and get some out. So you need to help me, OK?"

Jay chews his lip.

"You know—back-up, like Shaggy and Scoob on a secret mission."

"Partners," says Jay, grinning.

"Exactly."

I slip the letter under Nelly's door on the way out. There's no way my disguise would fool her X-ray vision from close range.

The moment we step outside, into the glare of the sun and the roar of the traffic, I freeze. I couldn't feel more exposed if I was naked. I stop at the bottom of the steps, fighting the impulse to bolt back inside and forget the whole stupid scheme.

"Nelly's coming," says Jay, glancing back up at the Heights.

I grab his hand and start walking. Nelly calls after us, but I pretend not to hear.

There's no money for bus fare so we have to walk all the way into town. I keep my head down, not looking at anybody. Jay's telling me about the episode of *Scooby-Doo* he watched this morning, blabbering on like normal. It helps. After a while I start to relax. I can do this. It's just like pretending to be Dad on the radio—I just have to get into character and believe.

I see the first kid from school as we cut down a side road towards the high street. A group of them, in Hardacre Comp uniforms, sauntering down the pavement ahead of us. It must be midday—lunchtime. I didn't realize it was so late. This is all I need. What if someone recognizes me?

Then I catch sight of myself in a shop window. It's a shock, but a good one. I don't look anything like me! I move closer to the window. The dark glasses really work: you can't see my face, and with the wig and everything, I look like a woman.

We wait at the crossing opposite the flower shop, Jay watching for the green man. It's busy—lots of people out on their lunch breaks, munching sandwiches, talking into mobile phones. I'm vaguely aware of kids in school uniform on the opposite pavement, waiting to cross, but I'm deliberately not looking at them.

Finally the traffic stops and the green man flashes up.

"Come on." I glance down at Jay. He's waving to someone across the road.

I look across at the crowd of people and see Mina on the opposite pavement. She's smiling and waving to Jay.

I realize I've forgotten one crucial fact: I might be unrecognizable, but Jay isn't.

It's too late to run. Mina is already crossing towards us.

"All right, mate!" She smiles and ruffles Jay's hair, then turns to me.

Her eyes boggle. "Laurence?"

Jay laughs. "He looks like Mum!"

Mina's hand shoots up to cover her mouth, then she leans forward and peers at me. "It is you!" She laughs, then stops herself. "What you doing? I mean, it's great—bit of an Eddie Izzard thing, yeah? Fair play to you—most blokes wouldn't have the nerve."

I don't know what she's talking about.

"You're not gay, are you?" she whispers. "Not that it matters. I mean that's fine by me, I just … well … " For once Mina seems lost for words.

"No. I'm not gay."

"We're going to the bank," says Jay in a loud voice. "They'll only give the money to Mum, but she's not here, so Laurence has got to dress up like her and pretend. I've got to be back-up, like Scooby."

This is why I'm not letting him go to school.

"What? Now I'm confused." Mina frowns and shakes her head. "Right! We need to talk. Come on, I'll buy you a cup of tea."

"We need to go to the bank."

"Dressed like that? Are you planning to rob it?" She raises an eyebrow. "You've got time for a cuppa, come on."

"I haven't got any money."

"I told you. I'm paying. So come on." Mina links her arm through mine.

"Where are we going?" says Jay.

"To the café."

"Brilliant!" says Jay. "I'm starving. We haven't had anything to eat for days!"

I wonder if I can gag him.

It's torture in the café. We're surrounded by food: the smell of it, the sound of it sizzling and spitting in the kitchen; there are even pictures of it on the walls. My stomach groans in awe.

"Right, what do you want?" says Mina, pulling out her purse.

"Just a tea, thanks."

"I thought you hadn't eaten for days?"

"He exaggerates," I lie.

"No I don't!"

"Bacon butty?" says Mina. "The Triple's good. Egg, bacon, and sausage. Want one of those, Jay?"

"I want chips and beans," says Jay.

"Just a drink, Jay," I hiss.

Mina turns to the woman behind the counter. "Two Triples and a plate of chips with beans, please." She turns back to Jay. "What do you want to drink, mate?"

"Coke!"

"Please." I give him a nudge.

"Please," Jay says, scowling at me.

"Tea? La...Lauren?" says Mina, a grin flickering in her eyes.

I nod.

"I'll bring them over." The woman behind the counter gives me a funny look.

As we cross the café towards a table in the far corner, I can feel people watching us. There's a group of mechanics in oily blue overalls at one of the tables. The oldest one of the group, overweight and balding, winks at me as we pass.

Mina thinks it's hilarious. Her shoulders are still shaking when we sit down, and there are tears running down her cheeks. It's hot in here; I'm sweating and the wig is itching like mad. I unzip Mum's jacket, too scared to take it off completely.

Mina's eye's pop. "You've got boobs!"

I shrug. "Bath salts. They aren't half uncomfortable." I rub my shoulders where the bra strap is digging in.

"Now you know what we have to put up with." Mina smiles. "So tell me again—why are you dressed like that?"

And there it is: the Million Dollar Question.

I could tell her the truth...about everything, but I still don't know if I can trust her. She's looking at me from across the table—it's that same look from the other night in the park, when she asked me why I ran off.

I'm saved by the arrival of the food. Jay cheers and claps his hands when the woman puts the plate of chips and beans in front of him. He drowns the lot in tomato sauce and starts shovelling it down as though he hasn't eaten for days—which of course he hasn't.

I smile at Mina. "Thanks. It's really kind of you … you know … to buy all this."

She shrugs. "It's what mates do, right?"

I nod and take a bite of the sandwich. Paradise unfolds in my mouth—soft white bread and butter, salty bacon and spicy sausage. Grease and egg juices run down my fingers and for a moment I can't speak.

"Told you they were good." Mina smiles, then her face goes serious again. "You still haven't answered my question. What's going on, Laurence? You've not been at school all week and the last time I saw you, you were sitting in a ditch. Today you're dressed up like a woman. Now, either you really are barking or there's a good reason for all this."

"He's not barking," says Jay, through a mouthful of chips. "He's Shaggy, *I'm* Scooby!"

Mina looks at him. "OK, I give in. You're both mad. I'm eating dinner with the Loony Brothers!"

"You're the loony, not us!" says Jay, frowning.

Mina laughs. "Is that right? I'm not the one dressed up with bath salts down my bra!"

"I told you!" says Jay. "We need to get some money so we can buy food. We've run out and Mum isn't here." He pauses, fork poised in mid-air, spilling a trail of baked beans onto the table.

I could jump in now and stop him. Shut him up before he tells Mina everything. But I don't want to. I want her to know. I can't carry the weight of the secret on my own anymore. So I take another bite of my sandwich and let Jay talk.

"Laurence has got to pretend to be Mum so they'll give him the money," says Jay, licking tomato sauce from his fingers.

Mina looks at me across the top of her mug. "Are you serious?"

I shrug.

"No offence, Laurence, but do you really think people in the bank are going to believe you're a woman, dressed like that?"

"It's the building society, actually."

Mina snorts. "Well, unless they employ blind people in there, it's still not going to work. You look like a bad drag act!"

"Well, what else was I supposed to do?" It comes out louder than I intended. I take off the sunglasses and throw them onto the table. I feel stupid dressed like this, and for ever thinking it was going to work. It also means we're back where we started: no money.

Mina doesn't flinch, just takes another bite of her sandwich and looks at me with those steady dark eyes of hers. She swallows and reaches for her mug.

"Where's your mum gone?"

I glance towards Jay. "She's away working," I tell her, while shaking my head at the same time.

Mina nods. "And you've run out of money."

"Yeah."

She takes another gulp of tea. "I'll lend you some. I went babysitting last night, so I'm loaded."

The offer is such a surprise, I don't know what to say. Then I shake my head. "Thanks, but it's OK, you don't have to."

"I know I don't have to, but I'm offering, so take it. You can pay me back, mind. If you don't I'll hunt you down for the rest of your days!" She grins.

"I can't take money off you."

"Why not? I thought you were desperate—you look desperate."

I shrug.

"If you go into the bank dressed like that," says Mina, "there'll be a police car waiting for you on the way out. I'm guessing that's not what you want." She nods towards Jay. "I'm guessing nobody knows you're on your own."

"Nobody."

Mina looks at her watch. "I should be getting back to school. Come on."

I drain the last of my tea and grab the remains of my sandwich—I'm not leaving that behind. We stand up and move towards the door and I catch the eye of the bald mechanic. He's grinning at me, his eyes glued to my bath-salt boobs.

"See ya later, darlin'," he shouts, winking at me again. His mates round the table are all grinning.

I nod. "See you, gorgeous," I say in my deepest voice, returning the wink.

His grin drops like a greasy chip from a plate. One of his mates starts to laugh. I give him a wave, then open the door.

Mina doesn't stop laughing until we reach the high street.

"I like you, Laurence Lauren Roach," she says reaching into her bag. "Never a dull moment with you!" Mina hands me a twenty-pound note. "Will that keep you going for a bit?"

"Don't you need it?"

"I was just going to buy something for Amy's birthday next week, but I can do it tomorrow."

I take the note. Suddenly my throat seems to have closed up on me.

"Right, I gotta go. Some of us have school to go to." She grabs my hand and writes on the back of it in blue pen. "My mobile," she says. "Call me, anytime. We need to talk, you and me." Then she reaches up and kisses me on the cheek. "Take care now, Big Man." She ruffles Jay's hair and walks away, waving as she goes.

"Why did she write on your hand?" says Jay.

I shrug.

"She's weird," he says, shaking his head. "I like her, though."

"Yeah," I tell him. "Me too."

"You know something, Dan, my friend," says Baz, "I'm going to miss you. We've been through a lot together, you and me—but like ALL good things it MUST come to an end. OF THAT WE CAN BE CERTAIN! The only thing we DON'T know is when. WILL it be tonight? Or WILL it be tomorrow?"

Baz pauses and the air crackles.

"TWO correct answers. ONE to go. Just ONE MORE question and you're THROUGH TO THE FINAL!"

Something outside the phone box catches my eye. A figure with long silver hair tied into a ponytail, crossing the car park. My heart bounces like one of Baz's stupid sound effects as the silver-haired man disappears inside Parade Wines.

What if it was Mum he was with that night? What if she's still with him? Waiting somewhere, right now. If I followed him, he could lead me to her.

"Daniel?" says Baz, in my ear.

"Yeah?"

"You still with us, champ? I thought we'd LOST you again."

"No. I'm here."

"Are you READY?"

"Yeah." My eyes are fixed on the doorway of Parade Wines.

"OK. Question number THREE. What is the name of the famous American landmark where the faces of former presidents have been carved into the hillside? Is it A: The Lincoln Memorial? B: Capitol Hill? Or C: Mount Rushmore? I'll read that again … "

The silver-haired man reappears with a red Parade Wines carrier bag in his hand. It's too soon! If he leaves now I'll never catch up with him. But instead of turning left, back towards the park, he walks along the Parade and pushes open the door of Choi's Fish & Chip Shop. There's a queue inside—I might just make it.

Except I wasn't listening to the question.

"Sorry, um, could you repeat that for me?"

"AGAIN!" says Baz. "That's HIGHLY unorthodox, but seeing as it's you…"

"Thanks."

"The monument in America, with the presidential faces carved into the side of the hill. What's it called? Is it A: The Lincoln Memorial? B: Capitol Hill? Or C: Mount Rushmore?"

"C—Mount Rushmore." I know this because I watched an episode of *Scooby-Doo* with Jay yesterday morning. The gang went on a trip to Mount Rushmore, and Shaggy and Scooby ended up being chased across the monument by ghosts of the presidents. Who says you can't learn anything from watching television!

"That's your FINAL answer?" says Baz.

"Yeah."

Inside Choi's Fish & Chip Shop, the silver-haired man is next in the queue.

"You're ABSOLUTELY sure?"

"Yes!" *Please get on with it!*

"I KNEW this would happen," says Baz. "I TOLD you we were going to have to say goodbye."

The chip shop door opens and a kid comes out, blowing on a tray of chips.

"MY FRIEND, I bid you FAREWELL. It's been great—what AM I SAYING? It's been a BLAST!" Baz is playing sad music with the sound of sobbing in the background.

The silver-haired man steps back into the Parade, carrying a Choi's Fish & Chip Shop carrier bag. It looks heavy. A takeaway for two? I have to see where he goes.

"Which is why," says Baz, "I'll be DELIGHTED if you would join us tomorrow night. SAME TIME—SAME PLACE—for the FINAL!" Wild cheering and firework sound effects almost drown him out. "When our reigning champion, DANNY THE ICEMAN Roach, will be just THREE questions—that's JUST THREE questions, folks!—away from winning himself an ALL-EXPENSES-PAID holiday in the sun!"

The Hardacre Holidaze jingle rattles through the telephone as the silver-haired man leaves the Parade and walks towards the park. I've got to go.

"I'll be there," I tell Baz. "See you tomorrow." I put the phone down.

Jay is waiting outside for me. I lift him onto my shoulders and start to jog.

"Where—we going?" says Jay, steadying himself with handfuls of my hair.

"We need to follow that man. The one with the silver hair." I can see him crossing the park some distance ahead. We need to get closer, or we could lose him when he goes through the hedge.

"That's—the man—from—the fair," says Jay, bouncing around on my shoulders.

I grunt. It's hard to talk and run, especially with Jay's legs clamped around my neck.

"Why—are we—following—him?"

"I'll tell you later. Just watch where he goes, Scoob!"

"OK—Shaggy."

The silver-haired man disappears through the hole in the hedge. I put on a burst of speed, worried we're going to lose him. When we get to the gap, I lift Jay down and peer through. I'm just in time to catch a gleam of sunlight on silver hair, disappearing around the bend to our left. I lift Jay onto my hip and make my way to the concrete bridge. Our quarry is almost at the lock, silhouetted against the sky.

"Come on." I hoist Jay back onto my shoulders.

The silver-haired man pauses for a moment to talk to somebody on one of the canal boats tied to the bank. It gives us a chance to catch up—but I don't want to get too close. I don't want him to know he's being followed. At least it means Jay can walk for a bit.

Up ahead, the canal curves round through a short tunnel beneath a tall black railway bridge. The silver-haired man disappears inside.

"We need to get closer," I tell Jay. "Get back on my shoulders."

But Jay shakes his head. "It hurts!"

"We'll have to run, then."

"OK."

We start to run, but after a few meters Jay drops behind. I keep going. I can't lose sight of the man now.

It's spooky inside the tunnel; my footsteps slap back at

me off the curved roof, and I'm glad to be out the other side. There's a line of three boats ahead, moored to the bank. The silver-haired man is level with the first of them. He keeps going, past the second and on towards the third. I hang back, keeping him in view, and wait for Jay. I can see through the tunnel to the disc of blue sky in the center, but there's no sign of Jay. He's probably too scared to come under the bridge. I should go back for him.

The silver-haired man walks on, past the last boat.

Where's he going? I can't follow much further, not without Jay.

I knew I should have carried him.

There's a second lock just ahead. The silver-haired man climbs onto the gate and crosses to the other side, then heads back towards the railway bridge on the opposite bank. I keep walking, so it's not too obvious I'm following him. There's a point when we draw level, separated only by the width of the canal. He looks across at me and nods. I walk on, waiting until I'm almost past the lock before turning to watch where he goes.

There's a boat, hidden from view until now by the overhanging branches of a willow tree. A short gray craft with a square cabin and round portholes; nothing like the brightly painted canal boats we passed earlier. A faint yellow glow illuminates the windows, and I can see blue smoke curling from the stub of chimney on the roof.

And I know straight away—

She's in there.

The feeling is like a blast of heat—so intense that when it's gone I shiver.

It was the same in the Tent of Mirrors and when I chased them through the park.

It's Mum. I can feel it.

I watch the silver-haired man climb aboard, then turn and run back towards the tunnel. Jay's waiting just on the other side. For a second he looks pleased to see me; then his face clouds.

"You ran off!" he says, on the verge of tears.

"Sorry, Scooby old pal, I had to follow the man. But I found out where he lives. It's a good job you were here keeping watch. Thanks, pal." I grin, not sure whether Jay is going to play along. "How about we stop for some Scooby Snacks on the way home? What do you think?"

I can see Jay is torn, caught between self-righteous anger and chips.

The chips win in the end.

It's cool and dark out here on the roof. Night rolling down its blinds on the day, filling the sky with stars. I can just make out the ragged line of trees separating the park from the canal. Somewhere in the blackness beyond is the gray boat.

Am I kidding myself thinking she's there? I've got no proof—just a feeling, fizzing like fireworks through my veins and telling me it's her. I need to be sure. And I have to do it soon—before my head explodes.

THISDAY

I'm up early, my brain still buzzing from last night. I want to get down there—I need to find out if it's really her.

"I'm not going to the stupid canal!" says Jay, fists balled.

"But we need to spy on that man, the one from the fair, see what he's up to. Come on, Scooby old pal—I can't do it without back-up!"

Jay folds his arms and glowers at me from under his blond fringe.

I don't know what to do. I can't leave him here on his own.

Then I realize the answer is staring me in the face— written in smudged blue numbers on the back of my hand.

I tell Jay not to move until I get back, and grab my phonecards.

Nosy Nelly materializes like an apparition when I'm half-way across the lobby.

"Good morning." Her eyes flick from me to the stairs. "Is your brother not with you today?"

"He's upstairs…" An alarm blares in my head, but it's too late to recall the words.

"Alone?"

"No! Mum's with him." *Idiot! What did I say that for?*

"Ah!" Nelly's eyes light up. "Excellent. I'll go and see her now."

"No!"

Nelly stops and looks at me.

"She's getting ready for work. She's got to go in a minute." My heart is hammering, making it hard to think. "Did you get her letter? She said she'll come and see you at the weekend—on Saturday."

Nelly sighs through pursed lips. "I'll expect her first thing Saturday morning. Nine o'clock sharp. Tell your mother I do not tolerate tardiness."

I'm engulfed by a choking cloud of old-lady perfume as Nelly leans towards me.

"But be warned. If I suspect for a moment that anything untoward is taking place upstairs, I will be informing the authorities immediately. Do I make myself clear?"

I don't say anything, just give Nelly a look.

But Nelly looks right back—

And it's me who breaks it off first.

"You want me to do what?" Mina sounds different on the telephone, more northern. "I'm supposed to be at school."

"Sorry... I forgot. Don't worry. It doesn't matter." I realize now it was stupid to ask.

I hear Mina chuckle on the other end of the line. "Didn't

say I wouldn't, did I? Just thought you might want me for something more exciting than babysitting your little brother."

My mouth goes dry. "Um ... "

"So, what are you doing that's so important?"

I hesitate, then tell her about Mum and the boat. And for a second there's silence at the other end. Then Mina speaks again.

"OK. Give me half an hour. I need to wait for Dad to go to work. Where do you live?"

"You know the shops? Parkview Parade. I'll meet you there."

I've never seen Mina not in uniform before—school or band. Today she's wearing a short dress covered in roses, a denim jacket, and huge white sunglasses. I notice that she's also wearing lipstick. She looks different ... very different ... and the Mina in my head is saying, *I thought you might want me for something more exciting ...*

"Thanks for coming over," I croak as she smiles and wheels her bike towards me.

"No problem, Big Man. Maths and double biology today anyway." Mina pulls a face. She looks up at the Heights. "So this is the place you haunt."

"Yeah. We better go in the back way."

Mina looks up at the fire escape.

"You might have warned me. I'm not exactly dressed for climbing!"

"Sorry."

She laughs. "Still, I should have known. If you're in-volved, it's bound to be something unusual." She touches my arm briefly. "I mean that in a good way."

Mina chains her bike to the base of the fire escape, then clambers up onto the bins behind me. "You sure this is safe?"

"It's been OK so far."

"Great! That makes me feel loads better." She grasps the rusty metal handrail and starts to climb. "No looking up my skirt!"

I turn my back and study the crumbling brickwork until I hear a shout from above.

When I get to the top, Mina is standing on the roof looking out across the park. "Great view. You can almost see our house from here."

I follow the line of her arm to a clump of trees in the far distance. She's standing very close and I can smell perfume; something light and fresh, nothing like the bug spray Nelly was wearing. I swallow and move away, suddenly conscious that I've been wearing the same pair of jeans for ... longer than I can remember, and that my T-shirt smelt bad when I pulled it out of the washing pile two days ago.

Jay's watching television; he doesn't turn round until Mina says hello. Even then he doesn't recognize her until she takes off her sunglasses.

"I've got to go out for a while," I tell him. "So Mina's going to stay with you until I come back."

"Why?"

"Because I can't leave you here on your own."

"Why?"

"Because ... "

"I wanted to watch some cartoons," says Mina. "We haven't got a telly at our house, and Laurence said you wouldn't mind if I watched some with you."

"You haven't got a TV?" Jay's eyes pop in amazement.

"Our old one blew up, and we haven't got a new one yet."

"Blew up!"

"Yeah! There was this big bang and loads of blue sparks. Frightened the life out of our cat!"

Jay thinks this is hilarious.

Mina turns to me. "Right, you better get going. Just show me where the kitchen is—I'm a bit parched after all that climbing."

I switch on the light in the kitchen and the roaches dart for cover.

"Whoa!" says Mina, grabbing my arm. "What was that?"

I'm looking around the kitchen—at the grease-stained cupboards, the piles of washing-up, the overflowing bin ... it's like I'm seeing the room for the first time, the way she must be seeing it. I've lived with it like this for so long it seems normal. Only it's not, is it? I wouldn't blame Mina if she turned round and left—jumped on her bike and never came back.

"Roaches," she says, after a moment. "My uncle had roaches in his shop—right little beggars to get rid of. Did you know they reckon cockroaches would survive a nuclear war?"

"No."

"It's true." Mina looks up at me. "So—you gonna get me that glass of water or what?"

I rinse a mug under the tap while my brain tries to accept the fact that Mina is still here.

"Are you sure your mum's on this boat?" she says.

"No, but I think she is. I need to find out."

"But why? I mean, why would she be there?"

"I don't know exactly… it's complicated." I hand Mina the mug. "Mum finds it hard … just living, you know? She gets depressed. Not just sad … but really bad, like she can't cope with anything. If she burns her toast it's like a major disaster." I shrug. "I think sometimes … being here, with me and Jay … it's too much for her."

Mina's eyes are dark and very still. I look away.

"She says drinking helps her feel normal. Sometimes it works. Sometimes she's really happy … only it's not like proper happy. It's all too much, like there's a big party going on that no one else can see. Other times she just gets angry."

"Has she ever gone away before?"

"She's stayed out all night a few times and once she disappeared for three days. Only that was when my Nanna was still alive. Someone found her passed out on a park bench and called an ambulance. The doctor said she was depressed. That she couldn't cope with her life, so she ran away."

"You think that's what she's doing now?"

I shrug.

"What you gonna do?"

"Dunno—make sure she's there first."

"Are you gonna talk to her?"

"Not today. I don't want to scare her off." I grin. "I've got a plan, see. If everything works out, I might have something that'll make her want to come home. But I won't know until tonight."

"Why, what's happening tonight?"

"Sorry, I can't tell you. Not yet anyway. If it works, I'll tell you then." I shrug. "It's been a secret all this time. I'm scared I'll jinx it if I tell someone."

"You're full of secrets, aren't you, Laurence Laurence Roach!" She raises an eyebrow. "So, who do you have to dress up as this time?"

I laugh. "No dressing up—I hope!"

Mina shakes her head. "Right, get lost then. My dad's back from work at six, so I'll need to be home by then."

"OK. It shouldn't take long. Thanks, Mina."

I've been sitting here for hours. Hiding in the trees above the canal, getting hassled by wasps, and gradually losing all feeling in my arse.

At least I've got a good view of the boat. In fact it's a perfect position, shielded from the opposite bank where the silver-haired man is fishing. He was there when I arrived and hasn't moved since. The trouble is, neither has anybody on board the boat. It looks deserted—no smoke coming from the chimney, no lights in the windows ... but I know she's in there. I've got that feeling again. It's so strong I can almost hear it—a low hum in the air, pulsing like a beacon inside the boat. But I want to see her. I need to be sure.

What if she stays in there all day? Mum can sleep for hours, especially if she's been on the booze the night before. I'll have to go soon, so Mina can be home before her dad gets back. I wonder how she's getting on with Jay? If I close my eyes I can see her standing on the roof in her rose dress... and something fizzes deep in my guts.

I open my eyes and see movement on the boat—the silver-haired man dropping his fishing tackle onto the deck. He opens the door and steps inside, reappearing a moment later carrying a black rubbish sack... and there, behind him, framed by the dark rectangle of doorway, the pale figure of a woman. I can't make out her features and I don't recognize the clothes, but it's Mum... it has to be. She hands the silver-haired man a red Parade Wines carrier bag and retreats out of sight. I watch as he crosses the lock and throws the bags into the trees on the opposite bank, then comes back and closes the door behind him.

I wait, heart-thumping, for something else to happen. If I could just get a better look, just to be certain. But I'm running out of time.

And then I get an idea.

It doesn't take long to locate the rubbish; it's obviously not the first time this place has been used as a dump. There are black sacks scattered all over the place. I find the Parade Wines bag half-buried in a clump of stingers and drag it out with a stick. Inside are three empty red wine bottles—Mum's favorite drink; a plastic tray with half a dozen shrivelled chips glued down with tomato sauce—Mum likes a lot of ketchup on her chips; and then, best of all, an empty, slightly soggy, gold packet of Benson and Hedges cigarettes. It's like looking through the contents of our bin at home, minus the cockroaches.

My heart is going so fast I feel sick.

I've found her.

I run all the way back to the Heights. I've been ages; Mina's going to kill me.

But when I get back, Mina and Jay are in the front room, drawing. The flat feels strange and it takes me a moment to work out why.

"What's wrong with the telly?"

"Nothing," says Mina. "We switched it off."

"We're drawing," says Jay. "Mina did one of me and you."

"It's not very good." To my surprise, Mina is blushing.

"It's brilliant," says Jay, snatching up a sheet of paper and thrusting it at me. "It looks just like us."

The picture shows a little boy in a baseball cap holding hands with a pair of giant legs and a T-shirt…

"I haven't got a head!"

"I ran out of paper!" Mina shrugs. "I was drawing Jay and he wanted me to draw you as well, but there wasn't enough room for your head. Sorry."

"Shut up! It's brilliant." Jay snatches the paper back. "Your face would spoil it anyway."

Mina laughs. "Laurence's face isn't that bad." Then they both look at me and frown. "Then again...maybe it is safer to leave it off...what d'you think, Jay?"

Jay thinks this is the funniest thing he's ever heard and rolls onto his back laughing.

"You're not funny," I tell them. "Either of you."

Mina grins and stands up. "Maybe now might be a good time for me to leave."

"Where you going?" says Jay, sitting up quickly.

"I've got to go home now."

"No!"

"I've got to. I'll get into trouble if I'm back late."

"No!" Jay grabs Mina's arm and tries to pull her back down.

"Jay! Let go!" I tell him.

He scowls at me. "No! It's not up to you!"

"I'm sorry, Jay, I really do have to go now." Mina crouches down next to him. "But I'll come and see you again, shall I? If Laurence says it's OK."

"It's not up to him!"

She smiles. "OK, I will then."

"When?"

"Soon."

"Promise?"

Mina glances up at me, then nods. "Promise."

"OK, then." He sighs and lets go of her arm.

Mina follows me down the hall. "So how'd you get on?"

I tell her what happened at the canal—the figure on the boat and the evidence inside the rubbish bag.

"Not much to go on."

I feel a prickle of annoyance. "It's her. I know it is."

Mina shrugs. "OK ... so what are you going to do now?"

"I dunno. That depends on how it goes tonight."

"Ah! The next secret mission. Are you sure you're not some kind of teenage spy or something?"

"Yeah, that's right, you've caught me. You better not tell anyone or I'll have to kill you."

"Fair enough, I suppose." She grins. "Right, I should be going ... before Dad gets home. I suppose you want me to go down the fire escape."

"No, you can use the stairs ... but do you mind if I don't come with you? If the woman downstairs sees us together ..." I shrug.

"Ashamed of me, are you?"

"No! It's ... "

She laughs and puts her hand on my arm. "Just messing with you, Big Man."

At the door, Mina stops and turns to face me.

"Good luck tonight, then ... with your secret mission." She grins, then stands up on her tiptoes and plants a kiss on my lips. It's so quick I hardly feel it.

"Thanks!"

Mina's eyebrows flicker. "You don't have to thank me, it was only a kiss."

"No, I mean…" I swallow. "You know… Jay. Thanks for looking after Jay."

"You're welcome."

I watch her cross the hallway to the stairs, where she turns and waves, grinning underneath those huge white sunglasses, and then she's gone. I close the door. Our flat has never felt so empty.

When the buzzer goes, I think it's Mina.

Maybe she's forgotten something, or just come back because… I don't think, I just open the door.

Angie from the House of Fun is standing there, wearing a huge yellow dress, beaming at me.

"Hello, Laurence love!"

What's *she* doing here? Then I remember the money we owe her.

"Is Mum about?" Angie looks past me down the hall.

"Mum's at work."

"We've not seen you and James for a couple of days," says Angie, easing her way into the flat.

It doesn't sound like a question, but it is.

"We were ill. Both of us. So Mum said we should stay at home."

Angie nods. Her eyes are everywhere. The door to Mum's bedroom is open, and you can see the stuff I tipped out all over the bed and the floor. I've got to get her out of here. If she finds out we're on our own, we've had it. Angie loves a crisis she can sweep into and sort out—somebody to save. But I don't trust her. She'd take over and ruin everything. In ways she scares me more than Nelly, because it's harder to stop people making you do things you don't want to when they're being nice.

Angie looks like she's about to say something when the door to the front room opens and Jay appears. He sees Angie and his face lights up.

"Hello, James!" Angie bends down and places a pink hand on Jay's sweaty forehead. "Ooh, you're absolutely baking, pudding!" She looks at me. "How long has he had this temperature?"

"Not long." I manage not to shrug. I didn't even know he had a temperature! But now she's mentioned it, I see how pale and pathetic he looks—standing there in his Scooby-Doo pajamas with jam stains down the front.

"Has he seen a doctor?"

"Mum's going to take him later, after work."

"I think she should." Angie turns back to Jay. "You're not a well bunny, are you, sweetie?"

Jay shakes his head and looks like he might cry.

"I could take him if it would help?"

"No! Thanks. I think Mum's already … you know, sorted it out … for later."

"Is Mum coming back later?" The surprise in Jay's voice is so obvious there's no way Angie hasn't heard it.

I give him my biggest plastic smile. "Yeah, 'course she is!"

Jay frowns and opens his mouth to speak. I hold my

breath, dreading what he might say, wishing I could get him out of here. Then the music starts—the familiar theme tune blasting out of the front room.

"*Scooby-Doo!*" Jay says, then runs back to the telly without even saying goodbye to Angie.

It's an effort not to laugh, I'm so relieved.

Angie knows the moment's gone, but she'll be back.

At the door, she pauses and gives me a long, meaningful look. "Laurence, if you need anything…someone to talk to…" She puts her hand on my arm. "You know where I am."

I nod and smile and say *thank you* about five times before she finally goes and I can shut the door.

For a few seconds, I just stand there with my eyes closed while the flat settles back into place like a bell after ringing.

Jay's the color of gone-off milk. His eyes are glazed and heavy, but he gets dressed so he can come with me to the phone box.

"You need me," he says. "For back-up."

He doesn't look great, but he's probably just tired. Angie likes to make a big deal out of everything. There's no way I'm taking Jay to the doctor. I don't know where the doctor is, for a start—but even if I did, it would be too risky—too many questions.

"SO," says Baz. "Here we are. Did you ever DREAM this day would finally come, Daniel my friend?"

"I've thought about it."

Baz laughs. "I BET you have! Are your bags packed?"

"Not yet."

"Very wise, my friend, VERY wise…because you're close. YOU—ARE—SOOOO CLOSE!" Dramatic pause—another Baz special. "But you're not there yet. If it was up to ME…I'd say HAVE the holiday! GO ON—TAKE IT! What's three extra questions between friends, eh? But I CAN'T. As I speak, Cheryl is waving the Baz's Bonanza BIG BOOK OF RULES at me—and BELIEVE ME when I tell you—it is ONE MIGHTY TOME! NOT a book you want dropped on you from a great height by your irate female producer." Baz laughs. "SO…for the sake of my personal safety if nothing else, Dan, I am going to ask you THREE more questions—and then YOU can get on with your packing and I can have a lie down! Because—I don't know about you, my friend—but I'm a WRECK!"

I laugh.

"Daniel, my friend…Shall we DO this?"

"Yeah."

"Good man. QUESTION number one—you're a cultured man, Daniel. How's your Art History?"

"Um…OK." I know nothing about art, but it *is* OK. I *am* feeling calm. If I don't know, I can guess. I feel lucky.

"WHICH artist," says Baz, "is credited—alongside Pablo Picasso—with creating the art movement known as Cubism? Was it A: Mondrian? B: Van Gogh? Or C: Braque?"

Van Gogh is the only one I've heard of, but that feels too easy, the one they always put in there to trip you up. So is it A or C? I don't know! My gut isn't telling me *anything*.

A line of cold sweat trickles down my back, and for the first time I feel a flicker of panic. Then I have an idea.

I clamp the telephone to my shoulder and nudge Jay. I hold out my hands—my left has one finger extended—my right, three. One or three—A or C? Jay looks at me and frowns.

"Pick one," I whisper.

Jay shrugs and taps my right hand—the one with three fingers out.

"C," I tell Baz.

"Daniel. We've been friends for some time now," he says, "and if YOU came up to me in the pub—and told me that PABLO Picasso and GEORGES Braque were responsible for starting Cubism—do you know WHAT? I'd believe you … because you would be ABSOLUTELY RIGHT, my friend!" The fake crowd roars behind Baz in the studio.

I let out the breath I was holding and give Jay a thumbs-up, but he's not looking.

"NEXT question. Staying on a cultural theme—though if I'm HONEST, this is more MY kind of culture!" Baz chuckles. "In the seminal, SUBLIME piece of animated television created by Mr. Joe Ruby and Mr. Ken Spears—WHAT breed of dog—is Scooby-Doo?"

I almost laugh out loud. I don't believe it! What are the chances? Do I feel lucky? Er … yeah!

Baz is doing a bad Scooby-Doo impression and going on about how he always fancied Daphne. Finally, he finishes the question.

"So, Scooby-Doo—what kind of DOG is he, Dan?

Your choices are: A: Great Dane? B: Doberman? Or C: Dachshund? Is that how you say that? Dachshund? Or is it Dash-hound? Cheryl?"

"Scooby's a Great Dane, Baz. A."

"ABSOLUTELY correct, my friend—of COURSE he is. Marvellous! Cubism to cartoons. You see—THAT's what you get on this show—the ENTIRE GAMUT of cultural experience!"

One question to go.

I shiver.

One more correct answer and I've done it. I've won the holiday. I can go and see Mum—tell her we're all getting out of here—a week away in the sun. Sorted.

"Here we go," says Baz, and in the background I can hear the start of "We Will Rock You" by Queen. I see a field full of waving arms, feel the thump of the drum in my chest and the movement in the air of a thousand voices chanting in rhythm. I'm floating, looking down on two figures in the crowd—a tall boy with his arms around a girl in a red and gold blazer. I'm overwhelmed by a sense of absolute calm.

I let the noise take me, high into the night, filling my lungs with ecstasy.

"Question NUMBER THREE. Sport."

Oh no!

"Daniel—which of the following—is NO LONGER an Olympic sport? Is it A: Beach Volleyball? B: Lacrosse? Or C: BMX Cycling?" It had to be a sport question. "Remember, Dan, we want to know which ONE of these sports IS NOT contested at the Olympic Games?"

Calm down, Laurence. Positive Thoughts. You feel lucky. Flying above the crowd—remember? Just work it out.

None of them sound like Olympic Sports to me, but then that's the whole point. It has to be BMX—that's the most ridiculous—so that's probably the trap. One of the others then—Lacrosse or Beach Volleyball? I'm not sure what Lacrosse is, but it sounds like it could be a sport. Beach Volleyball though? Where would they get the sand from?

"Daniel?" says Baz.

I'm trying to think, but there's nothing there—just a void, like my head is missing. Just like in Mina's picture.

"I'm going to HAVE to ask you for an answer, my friend."

"Beach Volleyball—A." *It's the sand. Where would they get the sand?*

The line goes quiet. For a moment I think I've been cut off again, then I hear Baz breathe.

"You SAID you were feeling lucky," says Baz. "You TOLD ME! *Baz, I feel lucky.* THAT'S WHAT YOU SAID!"

I've done it. I've won. He's just winding me up.

"Yeah," I whisper.

"You LET me down!" says Baz. "LACROSSE is the sport that WILL NOT be played at the next Olympic Games."

The sound of tumbleweed rolls through the Radio Ham studio and into my ear. I feel sick.

Baz is back at the mic. "But it's NOT over yet, boys and girls! Daniel got TWO questions right, which means our challenger will have to get ALL THREE—if he wants to take control of the *Baz's Bedtime Bonanza* Olympic flame. But CAN he do it?"

Keith, a software engineer from Hardacre, sounds nervous. He's struggling to get his words out and Baz is having to work hard to keep things going. I'm starting to feel better. All I need is for Keith to get one answer wrong and I've got a chance.

The first question is a hard one, but Keith doesn't even wait for Baz to ask it a second time before he fires back the answer. You can hear the surprise in Baz's voice, but he's pleased, too. This is perfect for them. Maybe this is what they wanted all along—for me to get right down to the last question. Just one question away from winning the holiday, and then fail. Bring somebody new in and the whole thing starts all over again.

I'm hardly listening as Keith answers question number two correctly. Baz is building him up now, reminding him that if he gets the next one right, he's won and I'm out.

I'm out.

Finished.

It's all over.

Suddenly I'm tired.

I just want to sleep.

Baz's voice seems to come from a long way away as he asks Keith his final question.

"In the cartoon series *Ben 10*, what SECRET organization is Grampa Max a member of? Is it A: The Agency? B:

The Plumbers? Or C: The Omnitrix? Are you a FAN of *Ben 10*, Keith?"

"N-no," says Keith.

A brief spark of hope glows in my chest.

"My s-son watches—it."

And dies again.

The answer is B: The Plumbers. I watch *Ben 10* with Jay. All the kids watch it. It's an easy question—everybody knows the answer.

Except Keith.

"C—The Omnitrix," he says, and I have to stifle a yelp of joy.

"Daniel," says Baz, "you TOLD ME you were feeling lucky—I SHOULD NEVER have doubted you! You're BACK in the game!"

Baz runs through the rules of the shoot-out again. If I answer this one, I've won.

"You know what," he says. "I'm not even going to ASK how you feel. I'm just going to read out the next question. That GOOD for you, my friend?"

"Yeah."

My ears are filled with the sound of pumping blood. I put my hand on Jay's shoulder and he reaches up and takes hold of my fingers. *Back-up*, I think.

"Daniel," says Baz. "Which of the following UNFOR-TUNATE creatures will not die—EVEN if you remove its head? Is it A: a crab? B: a cockroach? Or C: a chicken?"

What's that phrase—running around like a headless chicken? There was an episode of *Scooby-Doo* where Shaggy and Scooby were chased by a bunch of ghostly headless chickens—but that's not the answer. I know the answer. Even if I didn't, it's the one I'd choose. Because it's got my name all over it—

"A cockroach, Baz."

This time Baz doesn't do his silent thing, or his quiet voice like he's about to tell me I'm wrong. This time the phone explodes with cheers and klaxons, and Baz is shouting over the din.

"Daniel, my friend—it gives me GREAT pleasure—to announce that YOU—are the WINNER—of *Baz's—Bedtime—BONANZAAAAA!*"

I think he's waiting for me to speak, but I can't.

"One ALL-expenses-paid, LUXURY holiday for you and your family—courtesy of our friends at Hardacre Holidaze," he says. "It's yours, Daniel. Well done, my friend. VERY well done indeed."

"Thanks," I manage. Then I look down, just in time to see Jay throw up all over my foot.

FRIGHTDAY

The clock says 03:35 a.m. It's dark. No noise from outside.

Jay's sitting up in bed, wide-eyed and staring. He says he's going to school and he's all stressed out because he can't find his book bag. I tell him it's the middle of the night, but he's not listening.

"Where's Laurence?" he says. "I want my brother."

"I'm here, Jay." I put my arms round him, but he pushes me away.

"No! I want my brother!" He's looking right at me—his eyes are huge and full of fear. He doesn't know who I am and it's freaking me out.

Suddenly he lurches out of bed and staggers around the room.

It reminds me of Mum, drunk.

I guide him back and he lies there with his knees tucked into his chest, shuddering and staring at nothing. His face is slick with sweat, and I can smell the heat coming off him.

Angie said he had a temperature, that he needed to see a doctor.

I go into the bathroom and open the little cupboard

above the sink. Inside, next to the pink razors and an old toothbrush, are bottles of medicine and packets of pills. Most of them have got Mum's name on, and *NOT SUITABLE FOR CHILDREN* stamped across the label. I don't know what they're for and I'm not sure I could get Jay to take anything anyway. I'm wasting my time.

When I go back into the bedroom Jay looks even worse. His whole body is vibrating. It's like something in a cartoon—when Scooby-Doo gets scared and jumps into Shaggy's arms. He's shaking like crazy and you can hear this comedy bone-rattling sound—except this isn't funny.

What if there's something seriously wrong? Jay could be dying of some disease and I wouldn't know. What's that one they have the adverts for? Meningitis. How do you tell if someone has that? Something to do with a glass and spots … I can't remember!

I need to get help.

I could phone Mina—but it's the middle of the night. What's she going to do? Jump on her bike and ride all the way over here? And then what? She's not a doctor—she'll just tell me to call an ambulance.

There's no other choice.

I stumble into the hall and it's the glare of the light that stops me—the ordinariness of it.

If I call an ambulance that will be it—

The end of everything for both of us.

First the doctors—

Then the police.

There'll be no escape after that.

I grasp a lungful of air … and let it out slowly. I need to calm down.

But I shouldn't have to deal with this on my own. It's not fair! What the hell am I supposed to do?

I hear Jay coughing in the bedroom and remember why I'm standing here.

Shut up, Laurence! Stop feeling sorry for yourself.

I go back to the bathroom and splash some water on my face, and something in my brain makes a connection. Jay's hot—I need to cool him down. I remember Nanna fetching a cool flannel once when I was ill—laying it on my brow—how good it felt.

There isn't a flannel, so I get a wad of toilet paper and fold it over, then run it under the cold tap. The paper disintegrates in my hand.

I swear—and look around the bathroom for something else I can use. There's a towel hanging on the back of the door. I grab it and soak the corner with cold water, squeeze it out, then take it into the bedroom.

I sit on the edge of Jay's bed and lay the cool cloth on his forehead. He doesn't seem to notice me do it, just lies there twitching. He looks so frail with his dirty feet and skinny ankles sticking out from the bottom of his pajamas. Every breath sounds like there's something loose inside his chest.

If he gets much worse I'll *have* to call an ambulance—

But how much worse?

I don't notice the time, or the room starting to get lighter, until my stinging eyes flicker against the intrusion. I'm struggling to stay awake. My back hurts from sitting in one position for so long. I slide to the floor, resting my head on the bed so I can still hold the towel, and let my eyelids drop.

I wake up with the sun screaming through the window—heat sucking the air from the room.

Jay's asleep, and the towel on his forehead is completely dry.

My body is a bag of bones, my head made of dough.

I crawl over to my bed in search of sleep, but the room is too bright, too hot.

Then Jay wakes up and starts crying. His head hurts and he's got a tummy ache.

I try to give him a cuddle, but he pushes me off and says he wants Mum.

"Mum's not here." I lean against the bed, eyes closed.

"Where is she?"

Has he forgotten everything?

"I told you! She's not here."

I keep my eyes closed, but I can feel him looking at me, hear his rasping breath. "I want Mum."

"So do I." I open my eyes and the room flashes like a headache, so I close them again. "She's gone, Jay. She didn't want to be here anymore so she's gone. It's just you and me."

I can hear him, smell the staleness and bad breath coming off him, feel the heat of him beside me. It's suffocating.

He starts to cry quietly, sniffing between sobs.

Something snaps inside me.

"Oh, for God's sake!" I stand up and my brain knocks against the inside of my skull.

Jay looks up at me, his face a bloated ball of misery. I despise him for being weak and young and pathetic and ill—for causing me so much trouble. If I was on my own, I'd be out of here by now. If it wasn't for Jay, I'd be long gone.

His eyes are pleading, full of hurt and surprise, but that just makes it worse, makes it easier to walk away.

When I leave the room he starts to cry harder, louder. It tugs at the deeply rooted decency I'm trying to bury, but that only makes me angrier, more determined. I stomp around the flat with my fists clenched, teeth clamped together, breathing through my nose in tight, sharp bursts, but there's nowhere to go. No escape from the sound.

I need to get out—get away.

I make it as far as the door before it hits me what I'm doing.

Thinking like her.

Behaving like her.

I wake up on the settee with the TV blaring. My neck hurts. I sit up and every joint in my body howls.

Jay is at the opposite end of the sofa, cocooned in his

duvet. He still looks like one of the un-dead, but that's an improvement on earlier.

I stagger along to the bathroom and splash some cold water on my face. The puddle from the toilet is halfway to the door. I should mop that up … later. I wonder what time it is. How long I've been asleep. The sun is still trying to burn its way through the curtains, but it could be anytime. This day already feels like two. Maybe I slept through the night and it's tomorrow now. So what would that be, Saturday or Friday? Does it matter?

Something in the foggy depths of my brain is trying to fight its way to the surface. Something about Saturday … to do with Mum. Then I remember: Mum's meeting with Nelly. *Nine o'clock sharp.*

I stumble into the bedroom. The clock says 11:51 a.m. I've either missed it or it hasn't happened yet. I go into the kitchen and switch on the radio, but the noise is like needles jabbing at my brain. I turn it off and fill the kettle. Maybe some strong coffee will help.

I need to go back to the canal and talk to Mum. I've got to tell her about the holiday—get her to come home and stop Nelly from calling social services. But Jay's not well enough to go anywhere and I can't leave him on his own.

I'll phone Mina—ask her if she'll come and stay with him again. I'm halfway to the door before I remember that if it's Friday, Mina will be at school.

There's nothing I can do. Except wait. But I hate waiting. I feel trapped in here. Helpless.

I pick up the bag of shopping and hurry out of SavaShoppa. I only meant to leave Jay for a couple of minutes while I got some food, but there was a queue—I've been ages.

The sunlight drills into my brain as I step outside. I'm not looking where I'm going, my eyes half-closed against the glare, rushing to get back upstairs.

I don't see Angie until I almost walk into her.

"Laurence!" she says, sounding almost as surprised as I am. "What a coincidence! I was just popping up to see Mum. Is she in?" Angie starts walking up the steps towards the Heights.

"No!"

She stops and looks back at me with this weird expression on her face, smiling and frowning at the same time.

"Mum's out."

Angie walks back down towards me. "Not at school today?"

For a moment the sun glints off the gold crucifix resting on Angie's pink neck, blinding me. I'm the vampire again, cowering, stumbling away from the light.

"I wasn't feeling so good," I mumble. "Mum said to have another day at home." It's so obvious I'm lying.

"What did the doctor say?"

"Eh?"

"About James. Did Mum manage to take him last night?"

"Yeah! 'Course. Um…" I shrug. "A virus or something. Same as what I had. He's got some medicine."

"Jolly good." Angie smiles. "You're looking after him while Mum's out, then."

"Yeah! Just getting some food." I wave the bag of shopping as proof.

"How long will Mum be? Maybe I could wait. Pop up and see James." She starts up the steps again.

I can't let her back in the flat. There are too many lies holed up in there. Five minutes with Jay and she'll know everything.

"She's only just gone out. She'll be ages." I run past Angie so I'm between her and the front door.

She stops and stares at me—not smiling anymore. "Laurence."

"Yeah?"

"Is everything all right?"

"Yeah! Fine." My voice comes out all high and squeaky.

"You *would* tell me if anything was wrong, wouldn't you?" Angie puts her hand on my arm. It feels warm and slightly moist. My skin starts to sizzle.

"Yeah."

"I know Mum's had… problems." Angie's eyes bore into me. "I understand. I'm here to help."

I can feel my face melting. "Yeah. Thanks. But we're fine. Honest." I'm grinning, shrugging, and nodding, all at the same time. She probably thinks I'm having a fit.

Angie lets go of my arm and gives me a final meaning-ful look.

"Would you ask Mum to give me a ring later, Laurence love—she's got the number. I haven't seen her for such a long time. I think we need to have a little bit of a catch-up."

"Yeah. 'Course. Will do. Bye."

"Goodbye, Laurence."

She stands on the steps and watches me go inside.

So that's two of them now—closing in on us like a pair of perfumed Rottweilers.

TATTERSDAY

"What's that noise?" Jay looks up at me from the living room floor.

There's another thump on the door, followed by the buzzer. Two short jabs then a long burst.

"It's just Nosy Nelly. Don't worry about it."

"What does *she* want? Is she coming to look after us?" Jay's eyes widen.

I shake my head. "She just wants to talk to Mum."

"Oh," says Jay. Then he sits up. "Is Mum here?"

"No."

He slumps back onto the floor. "When's she coming home?"

"I don't know. Soon, I hope."

I haven't told Jay about Mum and the boat. I want it to be a surprise. Also, it's been two days since I went to the canal—I'm starting to worry that she might not be there anymore. All the more reason why we need to go back today. But first I have to collect the holiday—so we can give it to Mum when we get there.

We get the bus into town. Jay still looks like a ghost, but it's not a long walk to the radio station from the stop. I tried calling Mina, but her mobile went straight to voicemail. I left a couple of messages, but she didn't call back, so I had to bring Jay with me. It's already the afternoon. We're running out of time.

And there's another problem—a fatal flaw in my Great Plan. How exactly is the long-deceased Daniel Roach supposed to collect his prize? It's one thing impersonating a dead man on the radio; getting him to make a personal appearance is something else altogether.

For a while I toyed with the idea of dressing up, but somehow I didn't think I'd be convincing enough. *I'll dress up as my mum, but not my dad—work that one out.* So, after much deliberation and careful weighing up of the options— on the bus ride over here—I've come up with a plan ... sort of. It's so lame, I'm hoping it might just work.

We get off the bus and my stomach feels like a jar of wasps. The Radio Ham building is just across the road. I crouch down next to Jay so my face is level with his.

"OK, Scoob! This is a really important mission," I say, doing my Shaggy impression. "And I need you with me— for back-up! OK, pal?"

Jay stares at me. For a moment I think he's not going to play along, but then he nods and says "OK!" in his Scooby-Doo voice, which is surprisingly good.

"Great! Now listen—whatever you hear me say in there, don't worry, it's all part of the plan. But *you* mustn't say anything, OK?"

Jay frowns. "Why not?" he says, in his own voice.

"Because we don't want them to know who we are. This is a secret mission. Undercover."

"What's undercover?"

"Um … secret."

"You already said that."

"I know." I'm sweating and it's making my hair itch. "Look, just don't say anything—OK?"

Jay nods.

"Thanks, pal!"

I stand up.

This is never going to work.

The woman at the reception desk glances up as we walk in.

"Good afternoon! Can I help you?" She looks bored.

"Hello." I almost launch into my Scottish accent, then remember I'm not Daniel today. "Um … my dad asked us to come and collect his prize."

The woman's pencilled eyebrows concertina. "I'm sorry?"

"My dad—Daniel Roach. He won the holiday. On *Baz's Bedtime Bonanza.*"

"Ah!" She picks up a telephone. "What was the name again?"

"Daniel Roach."

She nods and punches three numbers with the end of her pen. "Hello? I've got Daniel Roach in reception. To collect his prize?" She nods, then puts the phone down. "Take a seat. There'll be somebody down in a minute."

There's a line of chairs with big square, squashy cushions against one wall, alternately red and blue—the Radio Ham colors. Me and Jay sit side-by-side underneath the framed photo of Baz. I was right when I guessed he was the one with the glasses, on the end. I wonder if he's here—if it's him that's coming down.

My heart is flapping around inside my rib cage like a trapped bird, and I'm sweating. It's stuffy in here, the sun roasting through the huge glass front of the building. There's a fan on the end of the desk, but it's pointing straight at the receptionist. I try to concentrate on the live radio feed coming through the speakers—it's a travel update—no problems on any of the major routes around Hardacre and Marston. That's good.

A door behind the reception desk opens and Cheryl walks through. I know it's her, even though I've never met her and she doesn't look anything like I expected. She scans the room and frowns. Then the receptionist points her pen towards me and Jay. Cheryl looks confused, but she smiles as she walks towards us. She's carrying a large gold envelope.

"Daniel Roach?" she says, looking at me.

"I'm Laurence. Daniel's my dad."

"Of course!" She shakes my hand and looks down at Jay. "And you must be James."

I'm impressed she remembers his name; I think I only mentioned him a couple of times on air.

Cheryl looks like she's expecting Jay to say *hello* or something, but I remember I told him not to speak.

"He's a bit shy."

"Not to worry." She smiles. "I remember Baz wanted to get him on the air that night."

"Yeah! He came down to help. He was my back-up, weren't you, Jay?" I put my hand on Jay's shoulder.

Cheryl frowns and I realize my mistake.

"I mean Dad's back-up—you know, both of us, like lucky mascots." *Concentrate, Laurence. Don't blow it now.*

"Well, it obviously worked!" Cheryl smiles, but she's giving me a strange look at the same time. "So, is your dad here?"

"No—he couldn't get out of work. He asked us to come down and collect the holiday for him."

"I see."

God it's hot in here.

"It's really nice to meet you, Laurence, but I'm afraid I can't actually give you the prize. We need your dad to come in and collect it in person." Cheryl gives me an apologetic smile. "The thing is, you see, we need to do some promotional shots with him and Baz—and the people from Hardacre Holidaze. This is quite a big joint promotion for us, and it's actually part of the deal."

I stare at her.

"I'm sure your dad won't mind," says Cheryl. "These things are normally quite good fun—and we can arrange a time that's convenient for him. Baz is actually really keen to meet him. We all are."

I nod. That could be a little difficult to arrange.

Maybe if I dressed up, or … what if I hired someone to pretend to be Dad? Mr. Buchan—he's got the right voice! But that's never going to happen, is it?

Face it, Laurence. This time it's just not going to work.

"Are you all right?"

"Yeah."

"No, I was talking to your brother. He's gone a funny color."

I look down at Jay. His face is white and shiny with sweat. He glances up at me, then lurches forward and vomits onto the red and blue Radio Ham carpet.

"Oh!" says Cheryl, stepping back just in time.

"Sorry!"

"Don't worry." She crouches down in front of Jay. "Shall I get you a drink of water, James? Would that help?"

He nods.

"Thanks."

She smiles and walks over towards the water dispenser on the far wall.

Jay's panting and swallowing like there's more on the way. Most of the sick has gone down the front of his T-shirt and shorts. It's pink and I can smell the strawberry jam he had for breakfast.

Cheryl comes back with the water. "There you go."

I take the cup and hold it up to Jay's mouth. He sips a bit and sniffs.

"Oh, look at his shirt," says Cheryl. "It's covered, poor lad."

"It's OK. I'll get him a clean one when we get home."

"Hang on!" Cheryl raises a finger and grins. "We've got some T-shirts left over from *Pop in the Park* upstairs. They'll probably be a bit big for him, but it should get you home."

"It's OK, honest."

"No!" Cheryl rests a hand on my shoulder. "You wait

there and I'll go and get you one. See if I can dig out a goodie bag while I'm there. Might help to cheer him up a bit."

"Thanks—that's great."

She smiles and disappears back through the door.

That's when I notice the gold envelope on the chair next to Jay. Just sitting there. Cheryl must have put it down when she went to get the water.

It's a big fat envelope. The shiny surface winks at me in the sunlight.

It's mine. I won it. It belongs to me.

"What are you doing?" says Jay.

The envelope is in my hands. I can feel the weight of it. There's more than just a holiday in here—it's the answer to everything. A way to get Mum to come home, and to make her smile again. An escape from the woman with the clipboard who's coming to take us away. It's our only hope. Our one chance and I have to take it now—before it's too late.

"Come on, we're going!"

"But what about the lady, she said … "

I scoop Jay into my arms, ignoring the sticky wetness and the stench of undigested food, then wedge the envelope between our bodies before turning towards the reception desk.

"I'm just taking him outside—I think he might be sick again!"

The receptionist nods, her face pinched in an expression of disgust.

I push the door, but it won't open.

"You have to pull it," calls the woman behind the desk.

I yank it open and we're out on the street. I don't look back. I just start running.

"I'm … going … to be sick," says Jay, bouncing up and down in my arms.

I don't stop. I don't care if he's sick all over me. We have to get away before somebody realizes what we've done.

Then Jay's sick all over me.

He starts crying. He's hitting me. He wants me to stop.

I turn up a side street and cross the road, ducking behind the row of parked cars. At the end of the road I turn right, then left. I don't know where I'm going. I just want to get as far away from the radio station as possible.

When I can't run anymore, I stop and let Jay down onto the pavement.

"Idiot!" he says, and kicks me.

I can't speak. My lungs are full of needles and my legs feel like they belong to somebody else. I check that there's no one following then bend over, gulping for breath.

Jay's sitting on the pavement with his back to me, sniffing and flicking lumps of sick off his T-shirt.

"I'm sorry, Jay. You OK?"

He shakes his head. He looks awful—sweaty and pale. There's no way I'll get him all the way to the canal now. Besides, we're both covered in sick. Perhaps not the best look for our great reunion with Mum.

At least we got the holiday. I wipe the half-digested strawberry jam off the envelope and tuck it into the waistband of my jeans. A corner of the cardboard digs into my chest, but somehow it's the best feeling in the world right now.

The golden envelope is in the middle of the kitchen table, propped up against Humpty. It's a bit creased and crumpled around the edges, but most of the sick wiped off OK. I feel bad about snatching it and running off. Cheryl was nice; she was helping us.

I did what I had to—that's all.

But what if she calls the police?

I only took what was mine. The envelope belongs to me.

Anyway, they don't know where we live, and there's no way they can trace us. Unless the police check and find out that Daniel Roach is dead. Can they do that?

But Cheryl knows my name—and Jay's. It wouldn't be that hard to find us. A few phone calls to the local schools ...

I look at the envelope, my face reflected as a dark shadow in its surface.

It could lead them right to us!

There's somebody at the door. The list of possible callers is getting longer: social services, Nelly, Angie, the police ...

It's OK, I don't have to answer.

The buzzer goes again. I ignore it.

Jay's in the front room watching television. He looks loads better, a different person than the wraith I took into town earlier.

"I'm hungry," he says, pulling a face.

I think about the perfectly good jam on toast he left on the carpet in Radio Ham. "I'll go and see what we've got."

"I want chips," says Jay.

"How about some toast?"

Jay shakes his head. "Chips."

"We haven't got any chips."

Jay shrugs his skinny shoulders and stares at the TV. "I want chips."

I can see where this is heading. I wonder if there's enough of Mina's money left for a bag of chips.

I'm halfway to the kitchen when I hear something—a hollow tapping coming from our bedroom. The frying pan is on the draining board—I grab it and tiptoe back into the hall. The noise goes again, pinging my heart. I take a breath and nudge the door.

Mina is waving at me through the window.

"I thought you were out," she says when I open it. "Thought I'd climbed all this way and risked breaking me neck for nothing." She hands me a heavy rucksack. "When you didn't answer the door, I thought I'd try the back way in!"

"Sorry! I thought you were ... well ... I didn't know it was you."

"I got your message," she says, grabbing my hand to steady herself as she climbs over the sill. "I had a gig, though. I couldn't get here any sooner."

"That's OK. It wasn't important."

Mina nods towards the frying pan in my hand. "So... you cooking?"

"What? No... I..."

"Oh, right! That's for me is it? Good job I knocked first."

I can feel my cheeks redden. "No! I thought..."

Mina laughs. "I hope you're hungry." She takes the rucksack from me. "There's half a ton of food in here—nearly killed me biking over. I'm not taking any of it home!"

I come back from changing my T-shirt—after a hasty wash and spray for my armpits—and find Mina out on the roof. She's laid down a large blue tartan blanket and covered it with food. There's plastic boxes of mini sausage rolls, bags of crisps, sandwiches, tomatoes, bright orange slices of carrot, and a huge bottle of lemonade.

Mina's standing at one end of the feast with her hands on her hips. She's wearing a black Ramones T-shirt and a pair of cut-off denim shorts. I can't stop looking at her legs.

"Wow!" It's the only thing I can think of to say. I'm talking about the food—mostly.

Mina frowns. "I think I got a bit carried away. I forgot I was going to have to lug it all the way over here."

"It's great!" Suddenly my throat is tight and for a horrible moment I think I might cry. I don't know where it comes from. Maybe it's just the sight of all that food—or the fact that Mina made it for us.

I try to bribe Jay with a plate of sandwiches and a bag of crisps in front of the TV, but he isn't interested. As soon as Mina says *picnic on the roof,* his eyes light up like she's just offered to take him to Disneyland or something.

I wedge him into the corner, as far away from the edge as possible, and tell him if he moves he'll have to go inside.

"It's not up to you!" he says, through a mouthful of crisps.

"Who is it up to, then?"

He points a stubby finger at Mina.

She laughs. "That's right, mate! I'm in charge!"

We eat and Jay talks—non-stop—pausing only to stuff more food into his mouth. It's the usual stream of disconnected nonsense: random thoughts mixed in with episodes of *Scooby-Doo.* For once I'm glad of it. It means I don't have to say anything. I eat until my stomach feels like a football, then sit back against the slope of the roof and close my eyes. I don't mean to fall asleep.

I wake up with a jolt.

"Back with us, then!" Mina grins.

"I just had my eyes closed."

"Right. So that wasn't you snoring, then?" She laughs and I feel her cool, thin fingers thread themselves through mine, sending a buzz of electricity sparking through my body.

"So, what happened the other night?" she asks. "Your secret mission—or are you still not allowed to say?"

I hesitate, out of habit, then tell her everything—about the quiz and the trip to Radio Ham, and finally about my plan to go back to the canal tomorrow.

"Wow!" says Mina when I stop talking. "That's quite a secret. You really are full of surprises, aren't you, Laurence Laurence Roach." She smiles, and her eyes are huge and dark.

"Hey, Mina?" says Jay.

"What's up, mate?"

"Was *Scooby-Doo* on TV when you were small?"

"Yeah! I used to watch it when I got home from school."

"Who's your favorite?"

Mina is still holding my hand, her thumb tracing a figure eight across my palm, over and over, making my skin hum.

"Scooby, of course," she says. "What about you?"

"Yeah, Scooby." Jay nods, his face serious. "I like Shaggy second, then Fred."

"What about Velma and Daphne?" Mina hooks her leg over mine and scrapes her foot along my shin. It's kind of painful, but nice at the same time.

Jay shrugs. "They're OK."

"Velma's the one who solves all the mysteries," says Mina.

Jay frowns as he thinks this one through. "Scooby helps, too. And Shaggy."

"Yeah, the whole gang helps."

Jay nods. "Do *you* want to be in *our* gang? Me and Laurence's?" He looks at me to see if this is OK. "I'm Scooby and he's Shaggy. You could be ... Velma ... if you want?"

Mina laughs. "I suppose I do look more like her than Daphne!"

Jay shrugs.

"You don't mind if I join your gang, do you … Shaggy?" says Mina, grinning. She squeezes my hand and scrapes her foot down my shin again.

It's getting dark. The heat of the day is finally fading and there's a faint warm breeze across the roof. For once the smell from the chip shop doesn't reach us and the noise from the Parade seems far away. Jay's dozing, curled up under his duvet in the corner. Mina is lying next to me, her limbs entwined with mine, her head on my shoulder. I can feel her breath on my cheek and her heart beating through my T-shirt.

As the light drains from the sky, the edges of the roof blur into the surrounding night. It feels as though we're floating, flying high above the town on our magic tartan blanket beneath a million shining stars.

SLUMDAY

The air is heavy and full of lazy buzzing insects. I can see the boat, tucked beneath its shady cave of overhanging branches, but no sign of any people. No Mum.

I stop at the lock.

"We need to go across here."

"Why? Where are we going?" Jay looks at the narrow gate, at the white apron of water flowing over the top into the canal below, and shakes his head.

I ignore the question and hold out my hand. "You'll be OK. I won't let you fall."

Jay takes a few steps back and folds his arms.

"OK, you stay here, but I'm going across."

His eyes widen.

"It's up to you."

I can see his mind working—his eyes darting down the towpath towards the gaping black mouth of the tunnel.

He takes a step towards me.

"That's it, Scooby old pal! You can do it!"

Jay grabs my hand and we step onto the gate, inching our way along as the water roars cold and chaotic beneath us. In less than a minute we're across.

Once his feet are safely back on dry land, Jay looks back at the lock.

"That was fun," he says. "Can we do it again?"

"On the way back, yeah."

"Now!" says Jay.

I shake my head and walk down the slope. There's no towpath on this side, just long grass and weeds, but there's a well-trodden path leading all the way to the gray boat. It's not much to look at. The paintwork is peeling and streaked with rust. There are holes in the side, with bits of wood nailed over the top. The whole thing is rotten and filthy—a floating version of the Heights. No wonder Mum feels at home here.

One of the windows is boarded up, and the others are covered with ratty bits of curtain, so I can't see in. But there's a faint haze of smoke coming from the chimney, which means there's somebody on board.

I tell Jay to stay where he is, then step forward and knock on the door. I wait—my heart hammering inside my T-shirt. There's no noise or movement from inside the boat. So I knock again.

This time I hear something—the murmur of a voice.

"What are you doing?" shouts Jay.

I'm about to answer him when I hear a cough and the clunk of a bolt. The door swings back and I'm face to face with the silver-haired man. He's wearing a faded denim shirt, unbuttoned to reveal a leathery chest thatched with wiry gray hair. There's a large bronze coin dangling on a chain around his neck, and his jaw is covered with gray stubble like iron filings. The smell of booze hangs off him like cheap aftershave.

"Who are you?" he growls, blinking at me through pale, watery eyes.

"Um…"

He leans out of the boat and looks down the bank towards the lock, then turns back to me. "What you doing here? I don't like kids."

"I've got a letter."

"A letter? You don't look much like a postman to me, son. What letter?"

"It's for… for Margaret Roach."

His eyes flash for a millisecond, no longer. But I see it all the same.

He shakes his head. "Who?"

"Margaret Roach."

"Never heard of her." He starts to close the door.

"She's my mum!"

The silver-haired man stops. "Say that again."

"Margaret Roach… she's my mum. She's on this boat."

He leans towards me. "Who told you that?"

"No one."

His eyes dig into mine, like he's trying to work out if I'm telling the truth. After a moment he grunts, so I guess he believes me.

"Well, I'm telling you, she ain't here. She's never been here. Understand?"

I nod. It feels like the safest thing to do. But I know he's lying—I can see it in his face.

Behind me, Jay suddenly shouts something and runs

towards the boat. He plants his hands either side of the nearest porthole and thumps on the glass.

"It's Mum!" he says, pointing at the window. "In there. I saw her!"

The silver-haired man looks ready to kill.

For a moment nobody says anything. Then we all hear the voice. It comes from the depths of the boat. Distant and drowsy, but loud enough…

"Phil? Who's out there? Who you talking to?"

My body jolts like a charge has passed through it.

"It's no one!" shouts Phil, his eyes fixed on me.

But Jay heard the voice too. He's beside me now, craning his neck to see into the boat.

"Mum!" he shouts.

There's a noise—a clatter of stuff being knocked over—then Mum floats up out of the darkness. Her face is a pale skull with sunken eyes; her hair, ragged and greasy.

"Mum?" Jay's voice is small and confused.

She stands at the hatch next to the silver-haired man and puts a hand on his shoulder to steady herself. She peers at us with a misty, bemused expression on her face, wobbling slightly. It's the Happy Hour Shake—she's drunk.

"Hello, Mum." The words scrape my throat.

She blinks at the sound of my voice and frowns. "Laurence?"

One word.

My word, on her lips, and it seals an aching hole deep in my guts and opens another in my chest. I feel heat slam into the back of my eyes, squeezing the tears out. I want to climb into the boat, jump into her arms, and weep. I want her to stroke my hair, kiss my face, and tell me that everything is going to be all right now. Mummy's here. All better.

"You've got kids?" The silver-haired man turns to Mum, but she doesn't seem to hear him. She's climbing out of the boat with this big dopey smile on her face. She laughs as she stumbles and almost falls over, then she's standing on the grass in front of us.

"My beautiful boys!" she says, her arms wide open.

Jay hesitates for a second, then rushes forward and flings himself at her. Mum drops to her knees and wraps him in her arms, laughing and hugging him to her. She looks up and holds out a hand to me—her thin white fingers trembling in the air. I'm scared to touch her, scared she won't be real. Then I reach out and she pulls me down, absorbing me into the crush of limbs, the smell of bodies and tears—and the sweet stink of booze.

Too soon she pulls away and sits back on her heels, her eyes shining. She looks at the silver-haired man watching us from the doorway.

"Phil, look! My boys!"

Phil grunts and starts to roll a cigarette.

"It's really you," she says, wiping at her cheeks.

"What are you doing here, Mum? Where have you been?"

For a second her eyes meet mine, then she turns to Jay. "Look at my Jay Jay! Haven't you grown!"

Jay grins. "We've been to the fair! Laurence's friend was sick! All down the man's back!"

"Mum." I try again.

"The fair! That's lovely!" says Mum, pulling Jay onto her lap.

"Mum! What are you doing here?"

Phil touches my shoulder. "Can I have a word."

I leave Jay talking to Mum and follow him along the bank.

When we're out of earshot, Phil stops and lights his cigarette. He blows a jet of smoke over my head, then offers me the tobacco. "Smoke?"

"No ... thanks."

"Good boy." He nods towards Mum and Jay. "She really your mum?"

"Yeah."

"Where's your old man?"

"My dad's dead."

"So who's looking after you?"

"No one."

Phil narrows his eyes. "No one?"

I shrug. "How long's she been here ... with you?"

"Couple of weeks." He takes a drag on his cigarette. "I pulled her out the canal, you know."

"What?"

"Yeah! Saved her life!"

My chest tightens. "When?"

"Couple of weeks ago. Lucky I heard the splash. Then

I see her come up over there." He nods towards the tunnel. "Thought I'd better go and pull her out."

I can't tell if he knows Mum was trying to kill herself or if he thinks it was an accident.

"Did you call an ambulance?"

"Took her back to the boat. Got her dried off, warmed her up. Then she crashed out."

"Why didn't you call an ambulance—or the police?"

Phil frowns. "Look, son! I told you—I sorted her out. It was the middle of the night. I let her sleep it off."

"And then what?"

"What do you mean?" His eyes darken.

"What happened the next day! She's been missing for two weeks!"

"Are the coppers looking for her?" Phil glances across the canal as if he expects to see lines of police converging on us.

"No."

He grunts and sucks on the cigarette, then suddenly his face changes. A moment ago I would have sworn he looked worried. Now there's something else, almost amusement. "You say she's been missing for two weeks and you ain't reported it?"

I'm not sure how much I should tell him, but then, I don't suppose it matters now. "Nobody knows. I didn't tell anybody."

The beginnings of a smile twitch the corners of Phil's mouth. "Why not?"

"Because if I had, they would have taken us into care."

"Ah…" He nods and flicks the end of his cigarette into the water.

"Didn't she tell you she had a family? Didn't you wonder where she came from?"

"What's it got to do with me? I told you—she never said she had kids."

I believe him.

"Anyway, I thought you said you had a letter."

I nod. I'd almost forgotten. "It's for Mum."

We walk back to where Mum and Jay are sitting together on the grass. I take the golden envelope out from under my T-shirt. It's even more battered now, but it still glints in the sun. It still sings like the magical thing it is.

Mum gasps and runs her fingers across the envelope. "What's this?"

"Open it."

She looks at me, then pulls up the flap and a glossy Hardacre Holidaze folder lands in her lap.

"It's a holiday. I won it. An all-expenses-paid holiday in the sun."

Mum turns the pages of the brochure in a daze, her head wobbling around like a bird's. I can tell she still doesn't understand.

"It's a holiday, Mum! A free holiday. You can go somewhere hot. It's all paid for. I won it. For you!"

Her face screws up in concentration. "A holiday? For me?"

"Yeah!"

Mum strokes the brochure with her fingers, like she's not sure it's really there, then looks up at Phil. "See what my boy's done!" Her voice is cracking and I can see tears in her eyes—just how I pictured it—sort of. She holds up the brochure like a trophy. "A holiday! A free holiday! We can go anywhere we want!" She turns back to me. "That's right, isn't it?"

"Yeah."

Phil gives me a doubtful look, then takes the brochure from Mum.

"We can go away, somewhere hot, by the sea!" Her eyes are gleaming she's so happy. "You could do with a holiday," she says, giving Phil's trousers a tug.

Something hard slams into my chest. "No!"

Mum looks at me.

"It's for us!"

She frowns.

"It's for us. Just me, you, and Jay." I look up at Phil and shrug. "I'm sorry."

He snorts and drops the brochure onto the grass.

The light is draining from Mum's face. She looks dazed, like she's just woken up and doesn't know how she got here.

"Mum? Are you OK?"

She pushes Jay off her lap and tries to get up, but stumbles and falls back onto the grass.

"I think you'd better go now," says Phil, helping Mum to her feet.

"What are you talking about? She's coming home with us."

Phil turns to Mum. "You want to go back with these two, Mags?"

She looks at me, and there are tears rolling down her face.

"Mum, please! We need you."

She's shaking her head, backing away towards the boat.

"Mum! Nelly's called social services. If you don't come back, they'll put us into care!"

She stops, but she won't lift her head to look at me. When she speaks, her voice is a whisper. "I can't. I can't do it anymore. I'm sorry!"

"Mum!"

The silver-haired man helps her into the boat, then turns back to me. "Looks like the lady wants to stay."

"But . . . she's our mum!"

He shrugs. "So what? You're telling me a big lad like you can't survive without his mummy—is that it?" Phil sighs. "Look, son—did you ever think why she didn't come home? Why's she's been here all this time? It's like she said—she can't do it no more. She don't want you . . . and neither do I."

He climbs aboard the boat and closes the door. I hear the click and rattle of a bolt being drawn.

I turn around, and Jay is standing there staring at the boat.

"Come on, let's go home." I hold out my hand to him.

"What about Mum?" he sniffs. "Is she coming?"

"No."

"Why not?"

I sigh. I wonder how much he heard . . . or understood.

"She wants to stay here for a bit longer, that's all."

"Why?"

"I don't know. She just does."

"Will she come home soon though?"

"Yeah! 'Course she will," I lie. "But until then it's just me and you, OK?"

We cross the lock and start to walk back towards the tunnel, Jay watching the boat all the way. "We'll be all right though—me and you," I say in my best Kid's TV Presenter voice.

Jay sniffs and nods. "And Mina."

"Yeah—and Mina."

"Our gang, like *Scooby-Doo*," says Jay.

"Yeah … something like that."

NONEDAY

Jay's moaning that he's hungry. He wants some breakfast. But there isn't any food left and we've run out of money again.

The gold envelope is on the kitchen table. There's a tear down one side now and grass stains to go with the sick. It's just a shiny envelope. It doesn't solve anything.

If Mum won't come home, it's over.

I've been thinking that Jay might be better off without me and Mum anyway. He'd get fostered in no time—a proper family, the chance of a normal life. Once I'm sure he's safe and happy somewhere, I could scarper. No one's going to bother too much about me. I can pass for sixteen, easy—get a job and a room somewhere...

I don't know if I've got the energy to carry on pretending.

The buzzer goes. I can hear muffled voices beyond the door—Nelly and someone else—a man. So they've finally come. Social services or the police? I don't suppose it matters much who it is. They knock, making the chain rattle. I wonder... if I don't answer, will they break down the door?

I sit on the lino at the end of the hall with my knees pulled up to my chest and wait. I watch the door, waiting for the noise—waiting for the paint to crack, the wood to split and buckle.

Nothing happens.

They've gone away.

I'm disappointed.

I go out onto the roof just in time to see Nosy Nelly emerge at the bottom of the steps by the Parade. She's talking to a man in a denim jacket—our Friendly Neighborhood Social Worker, it has to be. I watch as he shakes Nelly's hand, then climbs into a red Citroën 2CV and drives away. He's gone, but he'll be back.

I should get some things packed, clothes and stuff, so we're ready when he does. Maybe I should give Jay a bath and wash his hair. Nobody's going to want to take him smelling like he does now. My throat tightens like a fist at the thought.

Don't think, Laurence. Just do it.

I go back inside. I need to find a bag.

Two bags…

Just in case we don't end up in the same place.

"I hate baths!" says Jay, standing in the water, arms across his chest.

"I know, but we need to get cleaned up before we go."

"Go where?"

"We're going to go and stay with someone for a while. Just until Mum comes back."

Jay's eyes narrow. "Who?"

"I don't know yet, but they'll be nice." I try to smile, but my face won't cooperate.

I go and look for a towel. When I get back, Jay is sitting in the bath looking miserable.

"Are you clean yet?"

He shakes his head. "It's too cold."

I put my hand under the hot tap—the water coming out is icy. I swear and turn it off. "Wait there."

In the kitchen, I switch on the kettle. There's a bang—a blue flash—and the smell of burning plastic. I stand there for a moment staring at the kettle, then switch it off and on a few times, but the red light stays dark. Dead.

Something snaps.

Deep inside me.

Something I've been holding together for days…weeks… years probably.

Finally, it goes.

One moment I'm holding the useless kettle in my hand, and the next I'm on my knees in the middle of the floor— only there must have been an earthquake, because the kitchen seems to have exploded around me. The table is upside down, the bin on its side spewing rubbish. There are pock marks in the wall, little explosions of food, and splinters of crockery. I'm shaking, breathing hard through my nose, and there's blood coming from a cut across my palm.

Did I do this?

I get a flash of Mum all those years ago, in the middle of a sea of broken pigs…

There's a noise. I look up and Jay is watching me from the doorway, naked and shivering. He sees me and runs.

"Jay!" I stagger to my feet, rubbish squelching and crunching under my shoes. "Jay!"

I find him in the bath, frantically dragging the sponge across his body. He's crying and shaking. He won't look at me.

"Jay?"

"It's OK. It's not that cold," he says, the words wobbling through chattering teeth.

"Come on." I lift him out and wrap the towel around his body, then hug him to me. "I'm sorry. I didn't mean to frighten you. I just got … angry."

"I'm not clean yet," says Jay, sniffing in my ear.

"It doesn't matter. They'll just have to put up with us as we are, won't they."

He nods. "Where are we going?"

I rub his back through the towel and shake my head. "I don't know."

Our bags are ready in the hall. Mum's old green suitcase for Jay and a rucksack for me. There wasn't much to pack, and most of our clothes need a wash. I got Jay to collect his favorite toys, then put in as many as would fit.

There's a thump at the door. They're back. So this is it.

I walk down the hall and pause, my fingers touching the cold solid metal of the latch.

This wasn't how it was supposed to end.

But opening the door is easy.

Like letting go.

"So ... how'd you get on?" Mina breezes past me into the hall. "Fancy a chip? I bought an extra bag. Thought you fellas might be hungry."

"Mina!" says Jay, coming out from the front room.

"Hello, mate! Want some chips?"

"Yeah!" Jay claps his hands.

"Shall I get some plates?" Mina walks towards the kitchen, then stops in the doorway. "Blimey!" She looks at me. "What happened in here?"

I shrug and squeeze past her, picking my way through the debris.

"So ... how did you get on?" says Mina again. "Is your mum here?"

I shake my head.

"She's staying with her friend," says Jay, sticking close to Mina and the chips. "We're going to go and live with someone else for a bit."

"Great!" says Mina, frowning a question to me at the same time.

She tips some chips onto a plate and hands it to Jay. "Why don't you go and watch some TV, mate, while I talk to Laurence."

It's cool out on the roof; the air feels like cold water on my face.

"What's Jay on about?" says Mina, sitting down. "Where's your mum?"

I tell her about the disaster at the canal and my decision to give ourselves up.

"You're going to do what?" She pauses, a chip dangling from her fingers.

"What else can I do? We can't go on like this. Social services has already been round. They're going to find us in the end anyway."

"So you need to get your mum back here."

"I told you! She won't come."

Mina puts the chip into her mouth and chews slowly.

"You said she was drunk when you saw her?"

"She could hardly stand up."

"Well, there you go! Are you going to take the word of someone who can't even stand up? People do all sorts of things when they're drunk. Things they wouldn't do *or* say when they were sober. You know that!"

"I s'pose."

Mina sighs. "How many days has she been gone?"

"I dunno. Fourteen … fifteen."

"Two weeks," says Mina, waving a chip at me. "Two weeks you've survived—looked after Jay. All that, and now you're just going to give up?"

"I can't make her come home! Not if she doesn't want to be here!" The words clog in my throat.

Mina moves across to sit beside me and puts her hand on my arm. "It's not like that, Laurence. She doesn't know what she's doing. She's ill."

I stare at the floor, fighting the urge to cry.

"She's there because it's easy," says Mina. "When she's with this Phil bloke, she doesn't have to feel guilty—because he drinks too. She doesn't even have to think about it. That's why we've got to get her away from him. We'll go early—before she's had a chance to get drunk."

I remember the look in Mum's eyes as she backed away from me. "It won't work."

"God, Laurence! Listen to yourself. You're beaten before you start."

For some reason Nanna's face shimmers into my head—a projection from beyond the grave. She's got her stern face on, finger pointing. *Are you listening, Laurence Roach?* she says. *This girl knows what she's talking about.*

I look up at Mina and shrug. "OK. It's worth a try, I suppose. You're right."

"Finally, he understands!"

She grins, and for a second Nanna's holographic face smiles and winks, then pops like a bubble and disappears.

Nanna would have liked Mina. There's no doubt about that.

DOOMSDAY

It's early—just past eight. A layer of milky mist hides the surface of the canal, but it's warm already. There's nobody around, just me and Jay, our feet crunching along the dusty towpath.

"Shaggy?" Jay squints up at me from under the peak of his cap.

"Yes, Scoob?"

"Are we really going to rescue Mum?"

"We're going to try ... yeah."

Jay frowns. "Is that man ... the one with the silver hair ... is he a baddie?"

"Yeah ... sort of."

His eyes go big. "Is Mum in danger? Is he holding her prisoner?"

"No, but ... well ... we just want her to come home with us, don't we?"

He nods. "But how?"

"Mina's got a plan—I told you before."

"I forgot."

I sigh. "We're meeting Mina by the bridge ... "

"Velma."

"What?"

"Her name's Velma, not Mina." Jay shakes his head and tuts. "Look! There she is!"

He runs on ahead to where Mina is waiting, sitting astride her bike in a pair of cut-off denim shorts and a vest. There's an old leather dog leash draped around her neck.

"Where'd you get that?"

"We used to have a dog." Mina loops her finger through the end of it. "When he died, Dad couldn't bear to throw the leash away. It was still hanging by the back door." She shrugs. "You ready?"

I look past her towards the railway bridge in the distance—the tunnel like a mouth, waiting to swallow us up.

Mina puts a hand on my arm. "Don't worry, Big Man, it's gonna work. I can feel it in my water!"

"You what?"

She laughs. "Something my dad says. Now go! I'll give you ten minutes to get into position, then I'm coming."

Me and Jay are hiding in the trees where Phil dumped the rubbish, waiting for Mina. She should be here by now. Something's wrong.

Then I hear footsteps—someone running—and Mina flies past.

"Help! Somebody! Please!"

"Mina!" says Jay, his eyes big and white in the gloom.

I nod, watching as she crosses the lock. I can see the

boat from here, but the door is on the other side. Mina is still calling for help—it sounds so far away, almost drowned out by the blood thundering in my ears. Then everything goes quiet, except for the hum of flies and the distant hiss of the lock. And we wait.

And wait.

What if it doesn't work?

What if Mina can't get Phil away from the boat?

Then I hear voices.

I peer through the gap in the branches and see them—Mina and the silver-haired man crossing the lock. She's done it!

I pull Jay behind a thick tree trunk as they pass, less than three meters away.

"His name's Syd," I hear Mina say. "This big dog attacked him and then he ran off! And now I can't find him." She sniffs like she's been crying. "It was just down here—past the bridge."

Phil grunts and says something, but he's already too far away for me to make out the words.

I count to twenty before stepping out from the cover of the trees. We're just in time to see Mina and the silver-haired man disappear into the tunnel.

"Come on!"

We run to the lock, and this time Jay crosses without a

murmur—then we're down onto the grass, running towards the boat.

The hatch is locked—of course. I thump on the wood, sending a shower of paint flakes into the water.

"Mum! Open up! It's Laurence and Jay!"

The boat is silent. No movement inside.

What if she's gone?

I hammer again.

"Laurence!" Jay grabs my arm and points at the little round window in the side of the cabin. I catch a glimpse of a face before the faded yellow cloth drops back over the porthole.

"She's gone!" says Jay.

"No!" I go back to the door and start pounding it with my fists. The noise booms through the boat, rocking it in the water.

"Mum! Open the door! I need to talk to you!"

I'm beginning to think she's never going to answer—wondering if there's any way I can break in—when I hear a shout from inside and the door flies open.

I step back as Mum stumbles off the boat, shielding her eyes against the sunlight.

Jay runs up to her, arms outstretched, then stops, confused, as she raises her hand and backs away.

"What are you doing here? What do you want?" Her voice is ragged—harsh.

"We've come to take you home."

"Where's Phil?"

"He's gone."

"Gone? What do you mean?"

"Come on, Mum, there isn't much time."

"Where's he gone?"

"Don't worry about it. You're coming home with us." I look down at her bare feet. "Have you got any shoes?"

"What?"

"Have you got any shoes? Any stuff in the boat."

She's still looking for Phil—her eyes darting up and down the towpath.

"Mum, please!"

Jay grabs her hand. "Yeah, come on, Mum—we're rescuing you!"

She frowns and looks at him. "What are you talking about?"

"Mum! We've got to go!"

"Go where?"

"Home."

She stares at me, like I just said *the moon* or something. "I can't."

"Why not?" says Jay—

And everything stops.

No birds. No wind. No flies.

Silence.

Mum staring at Jay. Me staring at Mum.

Then Jay starts to cry. He just stands there—red in the face, mouth open, bawling.

Mum sinks to her knees and Jay flings himself into her neck.

"You see, I'm no good for you," she says, looking up at me. "I can't do it, Laurence. I always end up hurting you."

"You're ill, Mum. It's not your fault." My throat is tight. It's hard to get the words out. "It's not good for you here. You need to come home. We can help you."

She shakes her head. "It won't work, Laurence. You're better off without me."

"No we're not! We need you. They'll put us in a home!"

But she's not listening. "They'll find you a nice family. Somebody to look after you. Give you a proper life."

"No they won't! It'll be like last time."

"Oi!" The shout is distant, but I know who it is.

I turn in time to see Phil running towards us.

"What's going on here?" He stops, taking in the scene, then his head snaps back towards Mina crossing the lock. "This was a set-up! There never was a dog, was there! She just wanted to get me out the way."

He steps forward like he's going to hit me.

"Phil!" Mum gets to her feet. "Leave him! It's OK. They're going now."

"Not without you we're not." My voice is shaking.

Phil's hand comes up fast and I flinch, but he only grabs the front of my hoodie, squeezing the material into his fist, pulling me towards him.

"I told you—you're not wanted here!" I can feel his breath on my face; it stinks of cigarettes and stale booze. "Walk away now. You, him, and your little friend with the invisible dog, before—"

He stops. His eyes widen and he lets go of me, stumbling back. And that's when I see Jay—attached to the backside of Phil's shorts, growling through a mouthful of material.

"You little ... " Phil swears and swipes at him.

Jay rolls out of the way, then scrambles to his feet. He looks worried. Maybe he realizes that this time he really has bitten off more than he can chew.

The silver-haired man makes a lunge for him, but Jay is too quick. He's off and running, tearing past Mina up the bank towards the lock; I've never seen him move so fast. It's hilarious, watching the silver-haired man stumbling and growling after Jay—but he'll never catch him now. Jay's already on the gate, crossing the lock like an expert. He turns to check if Phil is still chasing him, and then—

One moment he's there.

And then he's gone. Just like that.

For a heartbeat nobody moves.

Then Mum screams, and I start to run.

Phil and Mina are ahead of me, both racing towards the lock. By the time I get up the bank Phil is already in the water, but there's no sign of Jay.

"Where is he?"

Mina holds up something dark and dripping. It takes me a moment to recognize Jay's cap. "This was in the water," she says, white-faced. "He must have gone under."

"No!" Mum pushes past and leaps into the lock before I can stop her.

She disappears in a plume of water, then surfaces, coughing and thrashing. Phil grabs her before she goes under again and starts dragging her towards the side.

I kick off my shoes.

"Laurence, what are you doing?" Mina grabs my arm. "You can't…"

I take a breath, then jump.

The water is colder than I expect. The shock punches the air from my lungs and I come up spluttering, my clothes water-logged and heavy, like hands dragging me down.

At the side of the lock Phil and Mina are trying to get Mum out of the water, but she's fighting them, screaming for Jay.

I'm on my own.

I gulp in some air and go under. The dark and the sudden silence is terrifying. I wave my hands blindly, groping into the murky depths—but there's nothing here. I twist around, battling the urge to swim to the surface, and kick down, scrabbling empty water. I can't find him!

My lungs are screaming. My heart ready to explode.

Then panic consumes me, shutting down my brain. I claw towards the light, but my clothes are too heavy, the current pulling through the gate too strong. I cry out and the water snatches the sound, forcing it back down my throat.

I'm drowning.

I'm going to die…

Then hands on my arm. Pulling me up. Into the light. And the air—

I cling to the silver-haired man, coughing and retching the canal from my throat, until I can speak.

"Where's Jay? Have you got him?"

Phil shakes his head and drags me over to the side of the lock where Mum and Mina are waiting.

"I can't find Jay!" I tell them. "It's too dark. There's too much water!"

There are tears rolling down Mina's cheeks as she reaches out to pull me up.

"What are you doing? I've got to find Jay!"

"No!" Phil grabs my shoulders. "He's gone. There's nothing we can do. That's twelve foot of water down there. You want to die as well?"

"I don't care! I'm not leaving him!"

I try to fight, but all my strength has drained into the canal. So I let them drag me out—onto the hard concrete at the side of the lock.

"Laurence!" Mum is crying. She kneels beside me, her hands reaching for my face, but I push her away.

"Don't touch me! It's all your fault!" I'm screaming, pointing at her. "It's your fault he's dead!"

Mum jerks backwards like she's been shot—

"No!" She whispers, shaking her head. "No!"

I turn away from her—and my body goes rigid.

There's a face in the trees on the opposite bank; pale and translucent, shimmering in the shadows—

Jay's ghost. Watching us.

It must be his ghost, because he's dead. I saw him fall into the lock.

Or did I?

Did anybody actually see him in the water? We were all too far away. What if he fell in, but managed to get out again—before Phil and Mina arrived.

I stare at the spectral face, scared to blink in case the vision vanishes.

I open my mouth to speak, but the words jam in my throat, so I grab Mina's hand and point.

When Mina swears, it breaks the spell.

Mum is the first to reach him. She scoops Jay up into her arms, then drops to her knees, sobbing. After a moment she pulls back and holds him at arms' length. "What the hell do you think you were doing?"

Jay blinks, his mouth open in surprise.

"I thought you were dead!" Mum shouts—then hugs him again, stroking his hair and kissing his face, over and over.

Jay looks up at me.

"Didn't you see me in the water?" I ask him. "I nearly drowned looking for you!"

He nods.

"Why didn't you shout?"

Jay looks over my shoulder, towards Phil—and all at once I understand. Jay was running away from Phil—being chased by the baddie. He fell in the water but managed to get out.

He must have seen Phil coming—still chasing him as far as Jay was concerned—so he ran and hid in the trees.

I kneel down and pull him towards me. "Idiot!" I whisper, kissing him on the head.

"*You're* the idiot," he mumbles back, and starts to cry.

I can't believe I'm sitting on the grass next to the canal, drinking tea. I'm wearing a pair of shorts and a T-shirt Phil lent me—Jay's got one too, only it looks like a dress on him. He's curled up on Mum's lap; she hasn't let go of him since we came down from the lock. Phil's leaning back against his boat, smoking and not saying much. Mina's next to me. In her shorts and vest she looks like she's just out for a picnic. I suppose we all do, except this feels more like the Mad Hatter's Tea Party.

The thing is, I don't know what happens next—and I'm too scared to ask.

Luckily, we've got Jay for that.

"I'm hungry," he says, looking up at Mum. "Can we go home now?"

For the longest time she doesn't say anything; she doesn't even move. In fact, I'm starting to think she didn't hear him—and then she nods.

"Yes," she says. "Let's go home."

Jay claps his hands and throws his arms around her neck. And that's it.

"Go and sit with Laurence for a minute," Mum tells Jay. "I need to talk to Phil."

I watch them walk along the bank, hoping he won't say something to make Mum change her mind.

Mina gives my hand a squeeze. "See—told you it would work."

"So that was all part of the plan, was it? Nearly getting everyone drowned?"

"Well, no ... not exactly." She shudders. "You're quite the hero though—diving in like that. Stupid—but brave. You know you're not supposed to dive in after someone, you're supposed to fetch a rope or a stick or something..."

I give her a look.

"Yeah, I know..." She shrugs. "Still ... it worked out in the end."

I watch Mum walking back towards us. She's smiling and Phil doesn't look happy.

This time, more than ever, I hope Mina's right.

I spot the red Citroën the moment we turn into the Parade.

Mum still seems to be holding it together, but this is just the kind of news that could plunge her back into the dark place.

"Mum! I think the social worker's here!"

She stops and stares up at the Heights—a giant tombstone casting its shadow over us.

As I'm wondering if we could all get up the fire escape and onto the roof, the door opens at the top of the steps and he's there—our Friendly Neighborhood Social Worker—with Nosy Nelly beside him, pointing down at us with a look of triumph plastered all over her face.

MADNESSDAY

"Mum! Wake up! He'll be here in half an hour!"

I go over to the window and pull back the curtains. The sun bangs on the glass like a leering rubbernecker, desperate for a glimpse of the horror inside.

Mum is facing away from me, her body twisted into the duvet, still wearing the clothes she had on yesterday.

She's been in here since we got back. I thought she'd go ape when she saw the state of the place—especially what I'd done to her bedroom—but she didn't seem to notice. Just floated around with this weird expression on her face, like she couldn't remember what she was doing here. An hour later I found her asleep, curled up on the bed in the middle of all the mess.

We were lucky yesterday. Our Friendly Neighborhood Social Worker said he'd just had an emergency call and had to go—but he'd be back to see us in the morning.

Which is today. He's due in half an hour!

"Mum!" I give her shoulder a shake. "Mum!"

I should really tidy up in here, but there isn't time. Mina thinks that the social worker bloke will want to have a look around, to check what our living conditions are like. Which is why me and Mina spent all evening trying to make the flat look like somewhere somebody might actually want to live.

The pan of water on the cooker is finally starting to boil. I put some instant coffee and two sugars into a mug for Mum, and some proper coffee, like they use in cafés, into another. Mina said the smell of freshly brewed coffee is homey and inviting; she saw it on one of those makeover programs on TV. I reckon it will take a lot more than the smell of coffee to make our flat feel homey and inviting, but it's worth a try.

I put the mug on the floor by the bed.

"Mum! I made you a coffee." I shake her shoulder again. "You've got to get up. He'll be here any minute. Please!"

"Go away. I'm ill." The voice is small, buried under the covers.

I was worried this would happen, once the shock of nearly losing Jay had worn off and the reality of being back here kicked in. But I won't give up now—not after everything we've been through—after everything I've done.

Mum told me once that when she's been drinking for a long time and then stops she feels terrible. It's like the flu, but much worse—and it lasts for days. The only cure is to have another drink. It works like a magic medicine—a few swigs and the pain goes away, just like that.

I fetch a glass from the kitchen and go over to the wardrobe. Mum's boots are still standing up in the corner. I hesitate, then reach inside and pull out the bottle of SavaShoppa

Scotch whisky. Whatever it takes … isn't that what I promised? I make sure the neck clinks against the glass as I pour.

"Mum." I lean over and waft the whisky towards her. "Have a drink. It'll make you feel better."

The shape in the bed doesn't stir.

"Mum! Please."

I listen to the distant babble of the TV while the smell of freshly brewed coffee drifts into the room. Fat lot of difference that will make if Mum won't get up.

Finally the twist of bedclothes rolls towards me and Mum's face, shiny with sweat, squints out through a letterbox of duvet.

"Why are you doing this?" Her voice is thin as burnt paper.

"What d'you mean?"

"You—giving me drink." Her eyes roll towards the glass. "You hate it when I drink."

I shrug. "The social worker's coming. I need you to get up."

My hand is shaking, sending ripples across the surface of the whisky. Then Mum reaches out and takes the glass. She holds it for a moment, staring into the liquid glowing golden in the sunlight, then drains the lot in a single gulp—and shudders.

"I don't deserve you," she says. "I don't deserve either of you." There are tears in her voice. I feel like I did all those years ago with the pigs, like I should put my arms around her or something—but I hesitate, and then the moment's gone.

"We can help you, Mum," I mumble instead. "We can help you get better."

She nods and looks down at the empty glass.

I pass her the bottle and she pours another measure, downs half of it, then refills the glass. If she carries on like this, she'll be drunk by the time the social worker gets here. But it's too late now. It would be like trying to take a bone from a pit-bull, getting that bottle back.

"Don't worry," she says, reading my face perhaps. "Just enough to get me through—yeah?"

I nod.

"Go on then!" says Mum. "Get lost while I get changed. Unless you want him to see me like this."

I'm in the kitchen when the buzzer goes. The flat shivers as the sound dies away.

"Mum! He's here!" I knock on the closed bedroom door. "Mum? Are you ready?"

Her answer is too muffled to tell what state she's in.

The buzzer goes again.

"I'm going to let him in."

I walk down the hall to the door and pause, my hand hovering over the latch.

Last chance to run. Over the roof and down the fire escape. We could still make it...

But I'm tired of running. Sometimes you have to stand up and fight. I glance back over my shoulder and there they are, the massed ranks of my army watching me from their doorways: a woman who can't get out of bed without the help of SavaShoppa Scotch whisky and a six-year-old boy who thinks he's Scooby-Doo.

I give them a thumbs-up and open the door.

Our Friendly Neighborhood Social Worker is called Chris. His face has a creased, weary look. He smiles and shakes my hand. I look round for Mum, but her bedroom door has closed again.

"Mum's just…" I shrug. "She'll be out in a minute."

"Great!" says Chris, following me down the hall. "You go to Hardacre Comprehensive, don't you?"

"Yeah." I'm wearing my school uniform—Mina thought it would give the right impression. For some reason I decide to wave my tie at him.

"I was talking to…" He frowns. "Mr. Duncan?"

"Buchan." A warning light blinks on in my head. How many people has Chris spoken to? How many lies am I going to have to remember? "Um…do you want a coffee?"

He looks surprised. "Yeah! That'd be great. Thanks."

We hover outside the kitchen looking at each other. I don't really want Chris to see we haven't got a kettle, in case this is on the list of *Essential Items for a Safe and Suitable Home*—but I'm not sure I want to leave him alone with Jay, either.

Chris makes the decision for me. "I'll go and wait in the front room, shall I?"

"OK." I can't exactly say *no*.

I'm just wondering whether I should call Mum again when the bedroom door bursts open and she appears in the hall.

She's wearing her interview suit—gray pinstriped skirt and jacket, black tights and a white blouse. She's done her makeup and put on a pair of high-heeled shoes. She looks...almost normal. A bit over-dressed, perhaps, but it's a magical transformation from earlier.

"What?" says Mum, shrugging.

"Nothing. You look nice."

She raises an eyebrow and looks past me towards the front room.

"Is he here?"

"Yeah. I'm just making some coffee."

She nods and glances back into the bedroom.

"You go ahead—I'll bring it in," I say, before she changes her mind.

"Yeah." Mum takes a deep breath. "Right. Here we go then..." She pauses. "Laurence...I'm not sure I can do this."

"You'll be fine." I smile, hoping she can't see how hard my heart is hammering through my clothes. "Just be...friendly."

Mum pulls a face, then nods. "OK."

"Mum."

She looks at me.

"Thanks."

She nods, half smiles, then totters down the hall towards the front room.

I pour the water into the mugs and stir, wishing that my hands would stop shaking.

"Do you want another coffee?"

"No, I'm good. Thanks, Laurence."

"Cake?" I thrust the plate of Bakewell tarts at him.

"Still OK with this one, thanks."

I'm beginning to think Chris is all right. He's nothing like the woman with the clipboard from the Dream. In fact, he doesn't act like a social worker at all ...

But he talks like one.

"You've not been at school for while?" He smiles as he says it.

"I was ill. We both were." I nod towards Jay, who is watching TV oblivious to everything.

"Sorry to hear that. How are you feeling now?"

"Fine. We're going back to school today."

"Excellent." Chris scribbles something on his pad, but I'm too far away to read what it says. He turns to Jay.

"And you've been unwell too then, James?"

Jay stares at the TV.

"Jay!" I hiss.

He looks up.

"Are you feeling better now?" says Chris.

Jay seems surprised to see him there—he frowns, then nods. "Oh yeah, I'm fine."

"You were too ill to go to school though?"

Jay shrugs.

"I don't think he remembers much about it," I tell Chris, before Jay says anything incriminating. "He was pretty much out of it for a couple of days. Didn't know where he was. Being sick and stuff, you know."

"Oh, yeah!" says Jay. "I was sick in the telephone box and in … that other place." He frowns. "With the nice lady. When we had to run away with the envelope so she couldn't give me a T-shirt."

My heart stops.

"Really?" Chris looks at me.

I force a laugh. "Jay was sick in this shop and the woman went mad, so we just ran!" I shrug.

"Where was Mum while all this was going on?" He looks across to Mum sitting rigid in a chair, clutching at the arms like she's afraid if she lets go she'll spin off into space.

I answer for her. "At work."

"Where do you work, Mrs. Roach?"

Mum looks at him.

"An office on the industrial estate," I tell him. "She's a cleaner."

"And at the chip shop," says Jay.

"Two jobs, then." Chris puts his pen to work again and turns to Mum. "That must keep you busy?"

Her eyes have gone glassy and her hands are trembling.

Come on, Mum, don't lose it now!

Chris is watching her, his pen hovering above the pad on his knees. There's a crumb of pastry from the Bakewell tart trapped between the wire binding holding the pages together. I tell myself that if the crumb doesn't drop, we'll be OK.

Mum blinks. "Yes, two jobs," she says.

Air rushes into my lungs.

"I need two jobs to pay for this place and keep food on the table. It's not cheap feeding these two, you know."

Chris nods. "Tell me about it! I've got two lads of my own, not much older than Laurence here." He smiles.

Here it comes.

"So you're out at work a lot of the time, then?"

I knew it. Act like we're just having a nice friendly chat...

"Not that much!" Mum's voice has an edge to it now. "They're not on their own for long, if that's what you're getting at? Anyway, Laurence is perfectly capable of looking after James for a few hours!"

Chris raises his palms. "I'm sure he is. I'm not *getting* at anything, Mrs. Roach. Nobody is accusing you, or the boys, of anything."

"Well, somebody must be, or you wouldn't be here, would you?"

It's like Mum's suddenly woken up. She reminds me of Jay—that same belligerent *it's not up to you* expression.

"It's that nosy cow downstairs, isn't it? I know it was her, so you needn't bother lying."

I wish she'd shut up. She's going to ruin everything.

Chris sighs. "I take it you're not on particularly good terms with Mrs. Ellison."

"You got that right!" Mum snorts. "She's been trying to get us out since the day we moved in. Didn't like it—me being a single mum. You could see it in her face, the stuck-up old cow!"

"Old cow!" says Jay.

For a second Chris looks surprised, then he laughs. You can see him trying not to, but he can't help himself.

Mum stares at him, black-eyed, ready to explode.

Then, out of nowhere, she starts to chuckle. You can feel the tension escaping, like the room has stopped holding its breath. Until Chris looks at his notebook again.

"Mrs. Ellison mentioned a flood...and a fire? She seemed to think the boys were here on their own when these incidents occurred."

Mum looks at me.

"There wasn't a fire." I try to put as much disbelief into my voice as I can. It's easier now. I get the feeling that Chris doesn't think much of Nosy Nelly. "I was making toast and it set the smoke alarm off—that's all."

Chris nods and makes a note. "Glad to hear you've got smoke alarms. And the flood?"

Nelly will have told him what happened. He's probably spoken to that bloke who was with her as well. Better to tell the truth or he'll think I'm lying about everything.

"We left the plug in and the sink overflowed. It was an accident. Anyway, it was only a bit of water, not a flood! She made out like her whole flat was underwater!"

"Yes, I must admit I wasn't overwhelmed when she insisted on showing me the damage." Chris shakes his head. "It's not as if we don't have enough to do without wasting time on petty complaints."

He closes the notebook. "Well, that about wraps it up,

I think. If you wouldn't mind just letting me have a quick look around."

The flat looks a lot worse than I'd hoped. You can tell Chris isn't impressed.

"How long have you been here?" he says, stepping out of the bathroom, where Mina's blue toilet liquid has only partially masked the smell of damp and wee.

"Nine months, give or take," says Mum with a shrug.

I switch on the light in the kitchen and a cockroach scuttles across the newly washed draining board, then disappears behind the sink.

"What was that?"

"Just a beetle," I say quickly. "We get them sometimes."

"Beetles?"

"Yeah."

Chris walks over and peers down the crack between the wall and the sink. "Are you on the housing list?" he says, craning his neck to see behind the cooker.

"No," says Mum.

"You'd be high priority, you know. Single parent, two kids. I'll have a word with one of my colleagues in housing."

Mum looks at him. She doesn't like being on lists. She doesn't trust colleagues in housing. But for once she doesn't say anything.

Chris opens the fridge door, and I'm glad I listened to Mina when she suggested we should get some food in.

Luckily there was some money in Mum's bag, so I went down to SavaShoppa and stocked up last night.

"This must be your room," says Chris, crossing the hall.

"Yeah, mine and Jay's ... we share."

He nods. "I like the stars."

"Yeah, Mum put them up. They're real constellations." I point up at the ceiling. "That's the Plough ... and that one's Orion ... only some of them fell down."

His eyes are everywhere, scanning the room for reasons to take us away. Then he looks at me and smiles, and there's an expression on his face that I can't quite read.

"Nice room," he says.

Chris is packing up his stuff, washing down the last of his Bakewell tart with cold coffee. Just a few more minutes and he'll be gone—and I might actually be able to breathe again.

Jay is still watching TV—now in his usual position, upside down on the floor with his legs up on the settee. His trousers have slid down to his knees, revealing skinny white calves and a purple bruise like a dirty handprint.

Chris spots it the same moment I do. He puts down his mug and leans over the chair. "That's a nasty-looking bruise you've got there, James. How did that happen?"

Jay looks up at Chris and frowns. He seems surprised to see the bruise. He shrugs.

"I did it when I bit the man to save Shaggy."

I stop breathing.

"What?" says Chris.

"*Scooby-Doo*," I croak. "We were playing *Scooby-Doo*. I'm Shaggy, he's Scooby."

Chris stares at me.

"Velma was there as well," says Jay. "The whole gang!" He grins and turns back to the TV.

My mouth has gone dry. "He must have bumped it when we were playing yesterday," I manage. "He crawls around a lot...you know...pretending to be a dog." I shrug, but it's hopeless. We're doomed.

Chris frowns and looks at each of us in turn: Jay, with the purple bruise like a tattoo saying *battered child*; Mum, by the window, cornered and ready to fight; and me— grinning and nodding like an idiot because I don't know what else to do.

"You know, my brother used to do that! Pretend he was a dog." Chris smiles and shakes his head. "He used to sleep in a basket on the floor at the end of his bed. Drove our mum batty!" He laughs. "He works as a dog handler for the police now. Loves it!"

I nod and smile and try to swallow the lump lodged in my throat.

Finally, we're at the door.

"Well, good to meet you all." Chris holds out his hand and we shake. "Back to school this afternoon?"

I nod.

"Good lad! I'll be checking!" He grins and turns to Mum.

"Thanks for your time, Mrs. Roach. All right if I pop back next week?"

"What for?" Mum's eyes flash.

"I might have some good news for you."

She shrugs.

Chris smiles and waves as he heads toward the stairs. "Take care now," he shouts, as Mum closes the door and leans back against the wood.

"God!" she says, closing her eyes. "I need a drink."

I can't get out of school fast enough. I shouldn't have let Mum talk me into coming back this afternoon. She'll be gone when I get home, I know it.

I'm halfway across the playground when I spot her—standing on the pavement outside the gate, smoking a cigarette. She's changed into jeans and a T-shirt and a pair of dark glasses.

"Mum!"

She smiles and drops the cigarette onto the ground, grinding it with the toe of her shoe. "I thought I'd come and meet you," she says, pulling the gold envelope from her bag. "What d'you say we go book ourselves that holiday?"

"Yeah…"

"I was just sitting at home," says Mum, linking her arm through mine, "and I thought, *This place is a dump! My boys shouldn't have to live in a place like this!* And then I found the envelope—the holiday you won for us. And I thought, *That's what we need—me and my boys—a holiday! Some time away from this place.*" She indicates Hardacre with a wave of her hand and beams at me.

Hardacre Holidaze is at the very top of the high street, severed from the rest of the town by the bypass road. All the shops up here have a dusty, abandoned look about them, like blackened toenails waiting to fall off. The blue sign above the travel agent's window, with its palm trees and cheerful yellow lettering, shines out from the gloom.

We wait to cross the road and I remember something important.

"Mum! When we go inside, don't say I won the holiday. You have to tell them it was Dad."

"What?" She frowns.

"I had to pretend I was him. You had to be eighteen to play."

"But why your dad? Why did you have to pick him?"

"It had to be somebody with our name." I shrug. "I'm sorry."

I push open the door, triggering a burst of Hawaiian music, and we step across the threshold into a fake tropical paradise. There's a photograph of a deserted golden beach filling one wall—with the words *Not just a holiday, the best daze of your life!* emblazoned across a cloudless blue sky.

An orange-faced woman dressed like an air hostess glides forward to greet us.

"Good afternoon. How can I help?" Her teeth, when she smiles, are so white I'd swear they actually light up.

"We'd like to book a holiday," says Mum, as if there's any other reason we'd be here.

"Do you have a destination in mind?" The woman shows us to a desk moored between two cardboard palm trees and we sit down on the plastic chairs in front.

"We want somewhere hot," says Mum. "Greece?"

"Greece is lovely." The woman taps at the computer keyboard in front of her. "We do package deals to Corfu, Thassos, Kefalonia, Zante…What kind of holiday are you looking for? Is it just the two of you?"

"No, three," says Mum.

"Four," I remind her. "Dad might want to come too."

Mum stares at me for a moment, then laughs. "'Course! How could I forget?"

"So a family holiday then? Two adults and two children?"

"That's right, the four of us. Your dad won't want to miss this one, will he?" says Mum, raising her eyebrows at me.

"And accommodation? We have a range of luxury five-star hotels, as well as spacious self-catering villas and apartments."

"Ooh, hotel!" says Mum. "I want looking after! Somewhere with a swimming pool!" She nudges me and winks. Happy. Enjoying herself.

The woman nods. "Let's have a look, shall we…" The sound of her nails clicking across the keys makes me think of the roaches in our kitchen.

"Here we are…" She turns her monitor towards us so we

can see the screen. "There's this one in Lyttos, Crete. Five-star, right on the beach. Five swimming pools!"

"Five!" says Mum.

"Or there's the Beach Retreat in Zante. Again, a lovely position ... they only have two swimming pools though."

"Bit of a dump, then," says Mum, laughing too loud.

The woman's face twitches. "Have you a particular budget in mind?"

Mum reaches into her bag. "My ... husband won this. It's all-expenses-paid."

Orange Lady looks slightly puzzled as Mum passes her the gold envelope. She takes out the Hardacre Holidaze brochure and the letter with the Radio Ham logo at the top.

"Ah!" she says, glancing at me, then back to Mum. "You must be Mrs. Roach."

"That's right."

The woman folds the letter and puts it back into the envelope. "I'm afraid we can't honor this."

"Why not?"

"It's been cancelled. The radio station reported it stolen." Her eyes bounce in my direction. "Apparently, two boys took it from Radio Ham reception at the weekend."

"Stolen!" Mum turns to me. "You told me you won it."

"Dad won it!" I'm aware that the woman is watching us. "Me and Jay just went to collect it. We didn't steal it."

Mum's eyes are boiling. "Why? Why did you do it?"

"I wanted you to have a holiday. Away from here—like you're always talking about. I just ... wanted you to be happy."

Mum erupts from her chair, sending it crashing behind

her, and leans over me. "You think stealing's going to make me happy?"

"I didn't steal it!"

I watch the skeletal finger trembling in the air, centimeters from my nose, and wait for the inevitable ... but it doesn't happen. Mum just lets out a long, slow sigh and turns back to the woman.

"Thank you for your help." She coughs and picks up the golden envelope from the desk. "Sorry if we wasted your time."

Orange Lady stares at us wide-eyed, her mouth slightly open like a fridge door, but she doesn't reply.

"Come on, sweetheart, we should be going," says Mum through clenched teeth.

I stand up and notice everybody in the shop is staring at us. I keep my head down and follow Mum to the door, wincing as the Hawaiian music heralds our departure. We stumble out into the street.

We wait at the bus stop in silence, Mum smoking furiously. I watch the rush hour traffic crawling along the high street and hear a burst of the Radio Ham jingle through the open window of a car. *Do I feel lucky?* Don't ask.

"I'm sorry ... about the holiday."

Mum exhales a lungful of smoke but doesn't answer.

"I didn't steal it, honest. It was mine—I won it. They just wouldn't let me have it."

She takes a final drag and flicks the butt into the road.

"Didn't want to go anyway—I mean, what's Greece got that we haven't?"

"Five swimming pools?"

Mum grunts. "Not much good if you can't swim."

"True."

"Anyway, if going to Greece means coming back orange like that stupid cow in the shop." She shakes her head. "That's a Hardacre tan if I ever saw it—straight out of a bottle."

I laugh. "Did you see her teeth?"

"Almost had to put my sunglasses on!" Mum's eyebrows flicker.

"We could still go on holiday, you know." My heart thumps. "I've got some money."

"Where'd you get money from? You didn't steal that as well?"

"Nanna gave it to me."

Mum looks down at her feet. "If you mean your building society—I spent it."

"You spent Jay's. Not mine."

Her head comes back up. "How much?"

"Enough … to go somewhere. Not Greece, but somewhere … by the sea."

"I don't know. That's your money, Laurence—what Nanna gave you."

"She wouldn't mind. She'd be happy if we went on holiday."

"Maybe … let's see how we get on, yeah?"

"OK."

She lights another cigarette, and I wonder how much

longer the bus is going to be. We need to get Jay from the House of Fun.

"I remember when you were born," says Mum, out of nowhere. "You were so small. Imagine that!" She laughs. "You looked so fragile, I was scared—scared I wouldn't be able to look after you." She sucks on the cigarette. "You used to cry all the time when you were a baby. All night sometimes. The people next door started banging on the walls, so I had to take you out—push you round in the pram. You'd fall asleep then, so long as I kept moving. I used to walk the streets for hours. Sometimes it would be getting light by the time we got home, but it was the only way I could stop you crying."

"I'm sorry."

She shakes her head. "It's not your fault, sweetheart. It was never your fault." Her bony fingers grasp mine. "It's me. I just didn't know what to do. Your dad left, and then Greg…" Another drag and a sigh of smoke. "When Nanna died I had nobody. I was on my own and I didn't know what to do." A tear trickles from under the black lens of her sunglasses.

"You're not on your own, Mum. You've got me and Jay." *For back-up*, I think, because Jay's not here to say it.

"I don't deserve you … either of you."

"You're our mum."

She takes off the sunglasses and wipes her face with the back of her hand. "You poor kid!"

"Yeah." I laugh.

"And you found me," she says, shaking her head. "I left you—and you came and found me."

"I only wanted to dump Jay on you—he was starting to get on my nerves."

She laughs—though it's part-laugh, part-sob, laughing and crying at the same time.

TODAY

The front door slams. Mum's back.

It sounds like a dead body hitting the ground as she dumps her stuff in the hall and goes straight to the kitchen. I hear the thud of a bottle on the table, the crack of the cap, then the slow glug as liquid spills into a glass.

It's been eighty-one days since Mum came home from the canal. Nearly three months. It feels like no time at all.

I leave Jay and Mina in the front room and go into the kitchen.

"How'd it go?"

Mum looks up through a doughnut of smoke, and sighs. "If there's anything going to make me want a drink, it's one of those meetings."

There's a yellow leaflet on the table with bold black letters across the cover: *Staying Sober—One Day at a Time.* It's been five weeks since Mum had a drink. As far as I know.

"What you got this time?" I pick up the bottle and read off the label. "Elderflower and ginger—any good?"

Mum pulls a face. "Tastes like someone washed their socks in it."

"Want a coffee?"

"No thanks, sweetheart. I've been drinking the stuff all afternoon." She leans back in the chair and her face brightens. "Jay didn't bite anybody at school today. Miss Shaw said they've got a chart for him, with stickers to put on each day he doesn't bite anybody."

I laugh. "He'll do anything for a sticker."

Recently, Mum's been collecting Jay from school...and taking him. She hasn't missed a day yet, this half-term.

"We could do one for you, if you like. You know, each day you don't have a drink..." I see the look on her face and stop mid-sentence, wishing I'd never started.

"Sorry! I..."

"It's all right." She shakes her head and looks away. "Might be a good idea."

Silence pours into the space between us while I try to think of something to say. Then Mina appears in the doorway.

"Hiya, Mags! Your hair looks nice."

"D'you think so?" Mum puts a hand to her head and frowns. "I thought I should get it done before I start. I couldn't go to work at a hairdresser's, the state I was in."

On Monday, Mum starts her new job as the receptionist at a salon in town. It's just part-time and not much money, but we're getting housing benefit now, thanks to Chris, and it's like Mum says: she won't come home stinking of chips, and she doesn't have to put her hand down anybody's toilet.

"It looks lovely," says Mina. "You don't look a day over twenty-five."

"I wish!" Mum taps ash from the cigarette, then tugs

at her lip. "I'm ever so nervous though … what if I make a mistake?"

"You'll be fine!" Mina walks over and gives Mum a hug. "Fancy a cuppa?"

"Ooh, go on then. Anything's better than this muck." She pushes the glass of elderflower and ginger across the table.

"Have you got your outfit sorted?" says Mina, carrying the kettle over to the sink.

"I keep changing my mind. Everything looks rubbish."

"Want some help?"

"Would you, love?"

"Of course. We'll have time before we go out. If the birthday boy doesn't mind." Mina looks at me and grins.

Today is my birthday. I'm sixteen years old.

"Happy birthday, sweetheart!" says Mum, placing the cake in the center of the kitchen table.

"What's that?" Jay stares at the plate.

"It's mine, you're not having any."

He looks relieved. "Why's it so flat?"

"It's great! Thanks, Mum." I give Jay a kick under the table.

It's the first time she's ever baked me a cake—even if it does look like roadkill covered in chocolate.

"Sixteen candles," says Mum. "Make a wish."

I look at the candles. At the cake. At the three faces watching me.

What do I want?

Not so long ago, that would have been easy.

Then a thought drops into my head and I smile. *Well, you never know ...*

"What did you wish for?" says Jay, tugging at my arm.

"No! If he tells you, it won't come true," says Mina.

Jay growls, then shrugs and hands me the card he made. He's been sitting on it—to make sure I wouldn't see—so it's a bit creased and slightly warm.

Happy 16 bithday Laurence!!! it says on the front, in a big cartoon speech bubble. Underneath Jay has drawn himself as Scooby-Doo, me as Shaggy, and Mina as Velma, and Mum ... as Mum. And at the bottom, in Mina's handwriting, *From all the gang!*

Inside there's another drawing of Scooby and something that could be a bone, or a telephone, with lots of splatters that look like blood.

"Scooby bit the baddie's leg off," says Jay, pointing.

"Thanks! That's ... brilliant."

"Yeah, I know. You can borrow it though ... 'cause it's your birthday."

"Borrow it?" I check to see if he's joking. "You know, normally when you give somebody a card, it's for them to keep."

Jay twists his mouth and shuts one eye as he thinks this over. "OK. You can keep it." He frowns. "Until tomorrow."

"You don't have to give this one back," says Mina, grinning as she hands me a red envelope. Instantly, my ears glow to match it. I'm relieved to see that the card inside isn't a picture of a pink teddy bear holding a heart-shaped cushion with the words *Happy Birthday to my Boyfriend* on the front—and a bit disappointed at the same time. Instead, it's a black-and-white photo of a bloke with boggle eyes and goofy teeth. Inside it says, *Happy Birthday Gorgeous.* Jay thinks this is so funny he falls off his stool.

Mum's clutching an envelope too. She thrusts it across the table.

"You already gave me a card," I say, then wish I hadn't. Maybe she forgot.

She's been forgetting lots of stuff recently. She says it's the pills the doctor gave her. Her Happy Pills, she calls them. She says they make her forget all the bad things that made her want to get drunk. Not exactly happy, then—but better than before.

Mum shakes her head. "It's not a card. It's … "

"A present?" says Jay, excited.

"I suppose."

I dig my thumb under the flap and tear it open. Inside is an official-looking letter with a small rectangle of plastic stuck to it. I don't know what it is, until I see the building society logo and my name, embossed in silver, across the bottom.

"What's that?" Jay looks disappointed.

"It's a cash card," says Mum. "So you can get your money out … whenever you want."

Jay tuts. "Boring!"

"No, it's not. Thanks, Mum."

She nods and for a moment her eyes hold mine. "I thought it might be useful. Now you're sixteen, you don't need me to sign for it anymore."

I know what she's thinking, but that's not going to happen.

I follow Mina down the stairs two at a time, our footsteps bouncing off the walls, racing us to the door. She's taking me into town to meet Han and Amy. It's a surprise for my birthday, so she won't tell me where we're going. We left Mum and Jay watching telly and eating my birthday cake, which tasted better than it looked.

A smell of cabbage and disinfectant hangs in the lobby like old curtains, but the door to Nosy Nelly's flat stays closed. Outside, the air is crisp and cool. I look out across the gray concrete sprawl of Hardacre and realize that right now, there's nowhere in the world I'd rather be.

The bus is already coming down the hill. I grab Mina's hand and start to run. I make a bet—if we get to the stop before the bus, then everything will be OK.

Even now it's hard to walk away, but every time I come home and Mum's still there, it gets easier. At least she's trying. Staying sober: one day at a time.

That's how we live.

We have good days and bad days.

But the gaps between the bad ones are getting longer—and that's something.

A good place to start.

We beat the bus by a car's length.

About the Author

Dave Cousins grew up in Birmingham, England, in a house full of books and records. Abandoning childhood plans to be an astronaut, Dave went to art college in Bradford, joined a band, and moved to London. He spent the next ten years touring and recording, and was nearly famous.

Dave's writing career began at age ten, with an attempt to create a script for *Fawlty Towers*. He has been writing songs, poems, and stories ever since. *15 Days Without a Head* was completed during late nights and early mornings and on lunch breaks from work, sheltering under a canal bridge when it rained!

He is now a full-time author and lives in Hertford-shire with his wife and family, in a house full of books and records, and writes every day in a corner of the attic with an anarchic ginger cat for company. Visit his website at www.davecousins.net.